The Caretaker

The Caretaker

{ A NOVEL }

Ron Rash

DOUBLEDAY   NEW YORK

All rights reserved. Published in the United States by Doubleday,
a division of Penguin Random House LLC, New York, and distributed
in Canada by Penguin Random House Canada Limited, Toronto.

www.doubleday.com

DOUBLEDAY and the portrayal of an anchor with a dolphin
are registered trademarks of Penguin Random House LLC.

Jacket painting: *Mountain View Cemetery,*
plein air oil painting by Karen Winslow
Jacket design by Emily Mahon

Library of Congress Cataloging-in-Publication Data
LCCN: 2023942792 (hardcover)
ISBN: 9780385544276 (hardcover)
ISBN: 9780385544283 (eBook)

MANUFACTURED IN THE UNITED STATES OF AMERICA
3 5 7 9 10 8 6 4

First Edition

For Steve Yarbrough

That world that opens up before you when a new sorrow enters your heart. Or you are shaken by profound music . . . Or when you see the miracle of the emerging new day. Then you know that we are strangers on this earth.

MARTIN A. HANSEN
The Liar

{ I }

1

J ACOB WAS ON GUARD DUTY, posted beside a river that
separated the two armies. The night was colder than any
he'd experienced back in Watauga County. This cold did
more than seep into his skin. It encased fingers and feet in
iron, made teeth rattle like glass about to break. No layering
of wool and cotton beneath the pile-lined parka allayed it.
For weeks Jacob had kept waiting for the cold to lift. Now
it was March, but this place observed no calendar. The
river was still frozen. Jacob envisioned ice all the way to the
bottom—no current, fish stalled as if mounted. The river had
a name but Jacob didn't allow it to lodge in his memory. Since
stepping onto the pier in Pusan, his goal had been to forget,
not remember.

At Fort Polk he'd heard all manner of stories about what
awaited him in Korea. Much of it was horsecrap: the NK
ate rats and snakes raw, could see in the dark like cats. But
some stories were true, including how they would crawl into
an outpost, slit a soldier's throat, then recede into the night.
Even if you were on the opposite side of a river, they'd come

across and kill only one man when they might have killed three or four. They were leaving a message: *We're saving you for next time.*

Though the river was frozen, Jacob knew that didn't matter. Two nights earlier, a North Korean had decapitated another unit's sentry. Crawled over the ice to do it. Jacob scanned the flat, soundless snowscape before him. At least the moon was full tonight. A hunter's moon, they called it back home. It silvered the crystals atop the river. If not wary of an enemy's knife, Jacob would have taken time to marvel at such shimmering beauty. But even this small moment must be blocked. Jacob wanted Korea to be a house entered and then left, the door locked forever. He just had to survive. Twelve days ago, for the first time, his unit had been in a fight. Aubert, a Cajun from Louisiana, had been shot in the leg. The bullet shattered his kneecap, and the medic said he'd need a cane the rest of his life. That was fine, Aubert answered. He'd get home alive to his wife and children, and finally be warm.

Getting home was what mattered. According to Naomi's last letter, Dr. Egan said the baby would come in May. That thought was the talisman Jacob carried with him. He could not die. God or fate, something, destined him and Naomi to have a life together. How else to explain that evening twenty months ago in Blowing Rock. At the exact moment he passed the Yonahlossee Theater, Naomi, a complete stranger, had been standing beside the ticket booth, coin in hand. If he'd looked up at the marquee, or if a friend had called from farther up the sidewalk, Jacob would never have noticed her.

She'd worn no earrings or bobby socks, no bright bows or bracelets like the other girls he knew. But such adornment would only distract from her face, the smooth skin and high cheekbones, striking blue eyes and long black hair. *Love at first sight.* But her prettiness was only part of what had held him there. As others went inside, Naomi rubbed a dime between her index finger and thumb, looking at the poster and then at the dime as people walked past her without a worry about the price.

So much in that instant was set into motion, including a shared life that ensured Jacob's safe return. Even Naomi being in Blowing Rock that July evening was little short of miraculous, Naomi's brother-in-law just happening to buy a copy of *The Nashville Tennessean* and noticing the ad: *Seasonal Hotel Maids Needed. The Green Park Inn. Blowing Rock, North Carolina.* Hadn't that been fate too? Many soldiers brought something from home to help protect themselves, a rabbit's foot, a lucky coin, a playing card, so why not a belief? Yet last week Doughtery, despite two crucifixes and a matchbox filled with four-leaf clovers, had stepped on a mine and been killed. So Jacob's eyes did not leave the frozen river, his ears listening for the rub of cloth on ice, a scrape of fingernails.

Most nights the wind howled across this hard country, but tonight a rare, disquieting silence. The rest of the unit was encamped fifty yards behind him, the chosenia trees muffling snores and dream mutterings. Did the North Koreans ever sleep? Perhaps all they did was wait until you did. The silence was palpable as the cold. Villagers believed the ghosts of dead Americans wandered these mountains. *Gwisin,* they called them. Most men laughed at the notion, but because of where he'd grown up, Jacob could not.

He wished he could smoke, but the flare of a match or

the glow of the lit tip might end your life. For an hour, Jacob
had barely moved. A slight shift of his rifle, a slow turn of his
head, but nothing more, as Sergeant Abrams advised. His
fingers searched for the pack of gum in his parka pocket, until
remembering he'd given it to a villager's child two days ago.
Jacob again looked up. Only the moon, not a single star. He
had the sensation that both armies had quietly withdrawn,
leaving him alone beside this frozen river.

Then, as if to signal otherwise, a movement on the opposite side of the ice. Jacob shifted his rifle, laid his gloved
finger inside the trigger guard. He watched the far bank, the
iced-over shallows. Nothing moved. After hours of guard
duty, a soldier easily imagined things, could even hallucinate.
Wind became whispers, shadows thickened into flesh. Jacob
resettled his finger on the stock. On guard duty the only thing
worse than being alone was the fear that you weren't. Sentries
had different ways to deal with that fear. *What works for me is
I tell myself that I'm not a man but a tree, and my heart is inside
the first ring in the trunk's center,* Sergeant Abrams had told
them. *If you stay rooted they'll look straight at you and see only
a tree. They can walk right past and still not know.*

Jacob imagined his and Naomi's farmhouse encircling
him. Beams and scaffolding first, then walls and floors and
windows, roof and porch. Every nail and plank in its proper
place, with Jacob in the center. *Heartwood,* sawyers called
center wood, and that was what protected him.

Jacob's eyes swept left to right. Back in North Carolina
he'd seen good-sized creeks cauled with ice, but never a whole
river. As he'd written Naomi, he hadn't known what cold was
until he'd come here. Or loneliness. He thought again of their

starting a family. Naomi wouldn't be eighteen until May. Although her sister, Lila, had her first child at seventeen, it still worried him. His parents could have helped. For a year after the elopement, he and Naomi had proven they could make a good life without any support from them. They'd saved enough money that when Dr. Egan said Naomi should no longer be lifting heavy objects, they could afford for her to quit the hospital laundry job. Then in December, with Naomi four months pregnant, the conscription notice came.

You swore you'd never come near this house again, his father had said as Jacob stood on the porch. His mother's footsteps echoed in the hallway. His father's hand remained on the knob, but he opened the front door wider so she saw who it was. On the mantel behind his parents was the prom photograph of Jacob and Veronica Weaver, the sole picture of him that hadn't been removed. Spiteful, but also as if to declare nothing could change unless his parents allowed it.

I know things haven't been good between us, but I want it to be different.

We told you how you could do that, his father answered, and you chose not to.

You're still my parents and I'm your son, and soon enough you'll have a grandchild.

His father's features altered into the cold smile of confirmation Jacob had known all of his life.

So this is about your inheritance.

No sir, it's not about that.

What then? his mother asked.

He hesitated, prepared himself for what would have to come first, the chiding certainty that if Jacob had only listened to them.

But Jacob already saw in his mother's face another kind of confirmation, that whatever Jacob was about to tell them would be bad.

I've been conscripted.

His father's hand slipped free of the doorknob. He appeared neither gloating nor aggrieved but stricken. His mother shook her head, kept on shaking it as she spoke.

Aren't two children enough to have lost? his mother implored, voice breaking as her arm gestured toward the cemetery where stones marked Jacob's sisters' graves. I will not hear this, she said, raising an open palm in front of her face. I will not. I will not.

She walked down the hallway to their bedroom and closed the door.

His father looked ready to follow her, then turned back to Jacob.

You can blame me for marrying, Jacob said. Maybe I should have waited like you told me, but being conscripted isn't my fault.

If you'd done what we told you, you'd have a college deferment, same as Doyle Brock's son, his father seethed, but like everything else you wouldn't listen, would you?

Jacob wanted to say no one, including his father, could know there'd be a war, but that would only make him more furious, more self-righteous and vindictive.

My being here, Jacob said as conciliatory as possible, it's not only about the conscription.

What, then?

It's about helping Naomi and the baby while I'm gone. However I've disappointed you, it's not their fault. I need you and Momma to check on Naomi, let her stay with you when her time nears. Despite all that's happened, it will be your grandchild, your blood.

What makes you so certain it is? his father answered. With that girl, I'd as likely it not.

Jacob had left then, driven down to Middlefork Bridge and parked. After a while, he'd turned around. Blackburn had been raking leaves in the cemetery. Alone, but his hat brim pulled low, as if even the dead might be frightened by his afflicted face. No one else will help us, he'd told Blackburn, so I've come to ask you.

Letting the M1 dangle in the crook of his right arm, Jacob clutched the parka's hood tighter. He bared a gloved wrist to check his watch, found comfort in the second hand's slow but steady circling, the tick of passing time. A few minutes more and Murphy would replace him. It was midafternoon in North Carolina. He imagined Naomi in front of the fireplace, half a world away.

As cold as he was, the enemy across the river was colder. Jacob had seen what their dead wore, the tan jacket with, at most, a sweater underneath. The jacket's material was as soft and pliable as the quilts that had covered Jacob on winter nights. He could see how some GIs believed the enemy tinctured themselves with quicklime and coal oil. How else to survive wearing so little?

On the edge of Jacob's vision a shadow shifted. He thumbed the rifle's safety and slowly turned his head. From the darkness a form lunged, a knife blade tearing through Jacob's parka, the tip raking his rib cage. He grabbed the man's arm, dropping the M1 as they fell to the ground, Jacob rolling on top. He reached out, felt his rifle's barrel and grasped it, only then realizing he hadn't fixed the bayonet. As Jacob's hand found the stock and then the trigger guard, the enemy soldier clasped Jacob's waist. They tumbled off the bank and onto the ice. It did not break and the landing knocked them apart. The M1 slipped free and skittered out of reach.

The North Korean wore only a sweater. He was shorter than Jacob but square-shouldered like a wrestler. His hand still gripped the knife. Both men panted, each breath whitening the air between them. Once their breathing steadied, they listened. Both banks were silent. Jacob jerked off his gloves, pulled his bayonet from its scabbard. Neither man tried to stand. They crawled closer, stabbing at each other, but the ice allowed little force in their thrusts, Jacob's even less so because of the parka. Then the other man crouched and sprang forward. His knife blade glanced Jacob's neck, drew blood. The North Korean's free hand slipped and he fell face-first, rising to his knees as Jacob's bayonet slashed his left cheek from ear to mouth, molars glinting white where the skin flapped open. One hand on the ice for balance, they swiped and jabbed, everything slow and unrelenting as a nightmare. Again they came together, arms entangled as they rolled onto their sides. Mid-river, they broke apart, each gasping for breath, each knowing a shout would bring fire from both shores.

On their knees, less than a yard apart, they saw each other clearly, the bright moon stage-lighting their struggle. The man's hair was long for a soldier's and he had to sweep it from his face. Dark smears marked their path across the ice. Most of the blood was Jacob's. The blood on his left hand had frozen, sealing the fingers together. Jacob flexed and unflexed a fist to free them. As the men watched each other, their breaths slowed. Jacob noticed a mole on the North Korean's chin, a bit of wool unraveling on his sweater. All seemed charged with significance. The soldier lunged, not to stab but to knock Jacob off balance. Jacob fell and the ice crackled. The other man was on top now. Jacob raised his left arm and their forearms locked a moment before the Korean's blade raked Jacob's wrist. Another stab sent the knife into Jacob's left shoulder and his arm went limp as more ice fractured. Jacob felt a sudden distance from everything around him, even his own heaving breaths. The bayonet slipped out of his hand. World and time unbuckled into a luminous vanishing, his body a burdensome shell so easily shed. *Let it all go, it won't hurt long.* But he could not let go of Naomi.

As the North Korean raised his knife, Jacob's right arm shoved the man off balance. The blade tip pierced the ice as Jacob twisted free. Inside the moon's circle of light, the soldier pried his knife from the ice and Jacob picked up the bayonet. Almost ceremonially, they knelt before each other. Their breathing slowed, widening the silence. Rising into a crouch, the North Korean slipped, fell backward, his flexed elbows breaking the ice and plunging him into the water. Half submerged but still wielding the knife, the man sought purchase, lifted one arm onto the ice, then the second. Jacob dropped his bayonet, crawled forward, and shoved the Korean under. When the head thrashed to the surface, Jacob, flat against the ice now, grabbed a fistful of hair and shoved harder, deeper. As he did, a spar of ice broke off beneath his right forearm. For a long moment, the arm, flexed rigid, hovered above the dark water. Time slowed more. Moonlight pressed against his back, as if it too had weight. Jacob eased the arm back. Sternum pressed against the ice, he tried not to breathe, but the pounding of his heart could not be stilled.

To be my heart that breaks it, Jacob thought, almost in wonder. The beating slowed. He tightened his stomach muscles,
lifted his arms and chest off the ice, breathed. He placed his
right hand beneath his stomach, pressed just hard enough to
raise himself and balance the weight between hand and knees.
He carefully turned, slid the bayonet into its scabbard, and
eased his body onto firmer ice.

Then Jacob heard a tick, and a second one. He looked
back, saw no movement on the bank. A third tick came and
Jacob realized that the sound came from downriver, and not
on the ice, but beneath it. Then the knife blade broke through.
It gleamed like a silver flame in the moonlight.

Jacob waited until certain the blade remained motionless.
Using his good arm for balance, he slid one knee forward,
then the other, making his way toward shore inches at a time.
For the first time he was scared. Jacob could almost feel a rifle
barrel steadying its aim on his back. He thought he heard a
whisper from the opposite bank. *Keep going,* he told himself.
They'll shoot whether you move or not. Jacob finally felt sand
and pulled himself ashore.

Someone whispered Jacob's name, then louder, more insis-
tent. Murphy's voice, but it came from the opposite shore, as
did a flashlight beam sweeping the ice. Above the bank where
Jacob crouched, there was movement. Two, maybe three
men. They spoke in Korean as their rifle bolts levered into
place. Shots rang out and were returned. There was an undercut in the bank. Tree roots brushed his face as he crawled
inside. After a few feet the undercut narrowed, came to an
end. Jacob pressed his back against the damp wall. The roof
rubbed against his shoulder and as he settled himself, bits of

dirt sifted down. Jacob smelled the earth's dankness. He wondered how deep the knife's punctures were, how much blood he had lost. To die here and never be found . . . Jacob tried not to think about what the villagers believed. Or of what he himself had witnessed back in Watauga County—ghost lanterns forever searching the flank of Brown Mountain. The shooting had ceased, but the North Koreans would be watching the river. *Wait until the moon is down,* Jacob told himself, *maybe then.* . . . But he was already drifting into unconsciousness.

2

WHEN REVEREND HUNNICUTT offered Blackburn the caretaker's position, his father had been against it, but his mother said at age sixteen Blackburn was old enough to choose for himself. He'd thought about it for a day and decided yes, mainly because he'd be around fewer people. Some in the community believed a sixteen-year-old would be too frightened to spend nights alone beside a cemetery. The old men who gathered daily at Hampton's Store agreed, though Brady Lister claimed one look at Blackburn's face would scare off any ghosts. Even on those first nights, however, Blackburn hadn't been afraid. The dead could do nothing worse to him than the living had already done.

Now, five years later, Blackburn sipped his morning coffee. He stared out the cottage window as the gravestones started to emerge, almost as if for a while they too had rested beneath the earth. Blackburn gaveled his fist against the table, tried to tell himself what had happened wasn't all his fault. Except for her doctor visits, he had kept Naomi out of Blowing Rock.

Shopping, paying bills, Blackburn had done all of that alone. Naomi complained about being cooped up, but winter's ice and cold offered a valid excuse. But two weeks ago a warm spell had come. When Naomi opened the door, instead of the maternity smock and saddle oxfords, she wore a blue-and-white dress and a pair of black wedged shoes. Two tortoise-shell barrettes swept back her black hair. It was Thursday, she told him, so there was a matinee at the Yonahlossee. Blackburn had tried to argue Naomi out of it, but she said Jacob knew how much she loved movies and wouldn't mind her going once before leaving for Tennessee.

He'd told her it was still chilly and insisted she put on her overcoat. As they'd driven toward Blowing Rock, Naomi opened her pocketbook and, looking in the side mirror, dusted her cheeks with powder, reddened her lips until they were bright as holly berries. When they turned onto Main Street, Blackburn pulled into a space in front of the movie house. Naomi began taking off her overcoat. *You ought to keep it on until you're inside, he'd told her. No, I want them to see my belly before I leave, she'd replied. They think they can shame me, but they're wrong.* Blackburn told her he couldn't let her go in like that alone because there might be trouble. *Then you come with me.*

Blackburn sipped more coffee. On the table before him, a cardboard box brimmed with what he'd take to Naomi in Tennessee. He checked his watch, saw it was already seven. Even if Blackburn left now, he wouldn't get back before dark. He swallowed the last of his coffee, raised his sleeve and wiped the drool from the corner of his mouth. Blackburn heard a vehicle. A humpback panel truck, *Dillard's Flower*

Shop painted on the side, pulled up in front of the cemetery gate.

Dressed in her wool coat and scoop-brim bonnet, Agnes Dillard opened the rear doors and removed a wreath and its metal stand. Blackburn put on his mackinaw and slouch hat and stepped out to meet her. She'd once told him that they were often much alike, both trying to ease people a bit during a hard time. There was always care in how Mrs. Dillard arranged flowers and wreaths. Blackburn saw it in details mourners might miss—how well woven the wreaths were or how stems were cut slantwise so flowers kept their color. He also knew that if he offered to place the wreath on the grave, she'd thank him for offering but do it herself.

"I told Mr. Burr's daughters that with this weather they ought to wait a couple of days, but it's his birthday so they insisted," she said as they entered the cemetery.

The grave was a month old. No marker, only a swelling of black dirt budded with hoarfrost. She pressed the stand's metal prongs into the frozen earth, mounted the wreath, and stepped back.

"With the wind I doubt it'll stay, but that's the best I can do."

As they left the cemetery, Mrs. Dillard paused and looked down the hill. The red Oldsmobile was parked beside the house, the same car Mr. Hampton had gotten out of two weeks ago, already yelling as he crossed Main Street toward Blackburn and Naomi.

"What Daniel Hampton said to that girl was disgraceful," the florist said. "She could of lost that baby because of such ugliness."

"I shouldn't have brought her to town."

"You couldn't know what would happen," Mrs. Dillard replied. "Anyway, she's better off with her family. You're about the only kindness that girl got around here."

"I hope she's okay there," Blackburn said.

"Have you heard from her?"

"No ma'am, but I'm going to check on her today."

"Think you ought to go?" Mrs. Dillard asked. "The radio says snow's coming."

"I'll be fine."

After Blackburn placed the carton for Naomi in the truck, he entered the cemetery for a final check, placed a vase upright, picked up a cigarette wrapper. Caretaking was a duty to the living and the dead. That was what Wilkie, the previous caretaker, had taught Blackburn. The placement of wreaths and flowers, the mowing of grass and raking of leaves, all must be done the right way. Wilkie was most adamant about properly digging and filling a grave—the exact length and depth, how soon before the service, how soon after. On the last day of Blackburn's apprenticeship, the old man showed Blackburn a trunk filled with the cemetery records and explained how to update them. Afterward, they'd sat at the cottage's one table, a leather-bound scrapbook between them. *What I didn't teach you is in this book, and you need to learn it all. People come here with their hearts grieving and they'll ask questions. It's a balm for them if you know the answers, confidences them that you'll take good care of their departed.* Blackburn had slowly turned the manila pages. At the back were pencil sketches of different-shaped stones, below each name, a sentence or two. Blackburn had never heard or seen words such as *discoid, volute, obelisk, fylfot*. Even ones he knew—*tree of life, compass star*—were strangely yoked.

Afterward, Wilkie took Blackburn into the cemetery a final time, paused before a marker in the back row.

SHAY
LEARY

The letters were wedged tight on a stone no larger than a salt block. Not a trace of moss or lichen clung to the marker. Killed by a dynamite charge while helping build the Blue Ridge Parkway, Wilkie told Blackburn. Fellow workers knew little about him besides his name and that he was from Ohio. Leary's co-workers bought the plot, chiseled out the name with a railroad spike. For two years nothing happened, but then one night the cottage's front door creaked open, slammed shut. Wilkie had gone onto the porch but found only darkness. The following night, though he'd latched the chain, the door opened again. Some kid playing a trick, he figured, so the third evening he set his rocking chair directly behind the door, waited with a shotgun to do some scaring of his own. When the door opened, no one was on the porch, but Wilkie saw a light hovering above Shay Leary's stone. Finally mustering the nerve, he went out to the grave. Before dimming, the light shone brightest in front of the lichen-hidden name. Come morning, Wilkie went to the grave with a wire brush and a cloth, made each letter distinct. On a rainy day a week later, he looked out the cottage window and saw a stranger. The man was Gabriel Leary, come from Ohio to find his brother's grave. He'd searched six cemeteries in this county alone, he told Wilkie, but now he'd finally found it.

A true story or told to ensure a new hire performed his tasks diligently, Blackburn did not know, but despite having had no such encounter himself, he nevertheless believed that in some way the dead sensed his actions, and not just the digging and filling of the graves. Small acts of respect mattered— not banging tools or talking loudly, stepping around graves not on them, picking up cigarette butts and matches.

Beside the cottage the weathervane creaked, swung as if opening the door for hard weather. Another day would be better, but Mondays were Blackburn's only full day off so he latched the gate, doubted it would be opened again until he came back. There were few visitors during winter. Those who came were usually widows or widowers. Sometimes he'd hear them speak aloud to the graves. According to Wilkie, Allie Higgins had come every week for eleven years. She'd stand beside her husband's grave and talk of daily matters, such as sewing and cooking, weather and gossip. The poor man never got a word in edgewise, living or dead, Wilkie had said in a rare moment of humor.

Blackburn cranked the truck and went down the drive, passing the turnoff to Reverend Hunnicutt's manse. At the bottom of the hill, Blackburn braked. Hampton's Store was across the road. Out front, an orange Gulf sign hovered moonlike above two gas pumps. Wind gusts made the round sign sway. Blackburn gazed past the Hamptons' two-story house to the pasture where one summer he and Jacob had fished for speckled trout in pools shadowed by rhododendron. Or, where the creek ran quick and shallow, flipped rocks to find what hid beneath—crawfish that raised pincers as they backed away, shiny-black salamanders that squirted through fingers before disappearing in swirls of silt. Sometimes under larger rocks they'd startle a water snake. Jacob tried to catch one once and it bit him, leaving a crescent of bloody dots. On those days whenever he and Jacob got hot and thirsty, Mrs. Hampton insisted Blackburn as well as Jacob take a bottle from the store's metal drink box. She never let Blackburn pay the few times he had coins to offer. Mrs. Hampton never smiled much, but she had always been nice. Until Blackburn started helping care for Naomi.

The road curved. In a half mile the Hamptons' sawmill came into sight, men in mackinaws and steel-capped boots sawing and planing trees into planks. The road dipped, following Laurel Fork Creek down the mountain. Blackburn crossed Middlefork and turned right. In a mile he turned again, soon came to Jacob and Naomi's farmhouse.

With its new tin roof and rebricked chimney, once boarded-up windows now glassed, the farmhouse was so different from eighteen months ago. Blackburn unlocked the door and stepped inside. The week after the elopement, Jacob and Blackburn went to Lenoir, first to a used appliance shop, after that a railroad salvage warehouse. *Disinherited,* gossipers claimed, and as Blackburn had watched Jacob haggle and check the bills in his wallet, he knew it was true. But money enough to fill the truck with a table and four rickety chairs, laundry tub, mattress and box spring, a battered dome-top refrigerator. So much of what made a house feel like a home had remained lacking, especially small things—

pictures, fireboard clock, kitchen calendar—but what he and Jacob brought from Lenoir that day had been a start. Now an armchair and davenport were added to the front room. On the fresh-painted wall a framed picture of a horse and sled, *Currier & Ives* written below. Beside the kitchen's new oil-burning stove, a Black Draught calendar already turned to August in anticipation of Naomi's return.

The photograph Naomi had asked him to bring was in the hallway. It had been taken in Lenoir on Jacob and Naomi's first anniversary. Blackburn lifted it from the rail hook, locked up, and drove west. In an hour, the road made a long ascent to the top of Roan Mountain. At a pull-off a man took pictures. Crossing into Tennessee, Blackburn remembered Naomi saying she'd thought that entering another state you'd see an immediate change, like on maps. But she'd found the trees and road and sky looked the same. Even the billboards, Blackburn thought as he passed a bright red Burma Shave sign, another showing a bottle of Royal Crown Cola. As the trees fell away and the land leveled, the billboards became frequent—Camel and Lucky Strike cigarettes, Ford and Lincoln automobiles, Sunbeam bread. On every face a smile.

3

D R. EGAN SAT AT HIS DESK, the pipe in the ashtray before him. At first, a prop used when he'd started his practice thirty-nine years ago. Egan thought its presence would help him appear older and wiser. Perhaps his early patients saw through the ruse, but as the years passed he'd kept his pipe, matches, and tobacco on the desk. It was here, in this room, that he brought those with the most serious maladies. Once the door was closed and both seated, he would light the bowl, draw in the smoke, and exhale. He'd set the pipe in the ashtray, the burning tobacco rising like a calming incense. *See, though we ponder serious matters, we will not be panicked.* A ritual not unlike the one he'd performed earlier today at Mindy Timberlake's house. For her, no cures lay in his black medical bag, yet as Mindy's three sons watched, Dr. Egan pressed the stethoscope's silver bell on the dying woman's chest. Right, up, down, like a priest's blessing. Minutes later she died, not with a gasp or rattle but a final soft sigh, as if some minor matter had been decided. A good death.

Dr. Egan looked out his window. Now mid-March, the

days were lengthening, so it would be a while before Blowing Rock's globed streetlights flickered on. Catherine's birthday was next week. He'd ordered the latest Erle Stanley Gardner novel but wanted to get one more present: maybe personalized stationery or a Parker 50 ink pen engraved with her initials. Yesterday, he'd peered into the window of Dillard's Flower Shop. When Egan had bought flowers for Helen, his late wife, they had always been red roses. However, a bouquet of roses might be viewed as a breach in the pact that he and Catherine had made. But chrysanthemums should be permissible. Yes, flowers and the novel would do fine. Catherine had once asked why he enjoyed poetry but didn't share her love of novels. *I spend my day immersed in stories,* he'd answered.

Including the one involving the Hamptons, Dr. Egan mused as he settled his eyes on Holder's Soda Shop. Daniel and Cora's consternation about Jacob eloping with a sixteen-year-old hotel maid was no surprise, their attempt to annul the marriage understandable. A year later when Dr. Egan confirmed Naomi's pregnancy, he'd hoped a grandchild might reconcile Jacob and his parents. But after what he'd witnessed in front of the soda shop, he knew otherwise. The girl had provoked not only Daniel but many in town with her lack of modesty. Egan wondered if the makeup and the dress were simple ignorance or spite. And what of Blackburn Gant allowing her to come like that? Either way, Daniel Hampton had no right to have said such terrible things. If Sheriff Triplett hadn't arrived, it could have ended much worse for all, including the baby. So despite the weather, Naomi's returning to Tennessee a few weeks earlier than planned had been the right decision. She was in her third trimester with no complications, he reminded himself. Still . . .

Dr. Egan wanted to be sympathetic toward the Hamptons. He'd witnessed Daniel and Cora's despair when their two daughters died. During the worst times of the Depression, the Hamptons had done much good when others with wealth had not. Nevertheless, Cora and Daniel made clear their status. Jacob wore proper short pants in the summertime, gloves and wool sweaters in winter. He was sent to Blowing Rock's schools to learn alongside the children of merchants and professionals. Considering everything, Jacob had turned out better than one might have expected. Impulsive—the dropping out of college and elopement were proof of that—but goodhearted, especially toward Blackburn Gant.

A quick tap and the office door opened.

"I'm about to leave," Ruthie said, and pointed at a note taped to the center of his desk. "That needs to be done before the pharmacy closes."

"Yes," Dr. Egan said, "I was just about to get to it."

Ruthie adjusted the bridge of her cat-eyed glasses, as she did when patients said something so outlandish that hearing and even *sight* might be doubted.

"I'm sure you were," she answered drily.

As the door closed, he took out his prescription pad, set Ruthie's note beside it.

Don't forget to write and fill Lee Barton's nitrite Rx!!! The punctuation of a no-nonsense woman who wore her bod-kinned hair in a tight bun more martial than decorative. Dr. Egan smiled. Ruthie had a Swiftian wit about her, and not always at his expense. When Darnell Wallace said he had no idea how he'd contracted gonorrhea, Ruthie told him to look between his legs for a clue.

Yet her considerable kindness revealed itself with children and elderly men. The latter reminded Ruthie of her grandfather, who'd taken in the family after her father died, one of the few personal details she'd ever disclosed. Yet there was an intimacy between them. They knew the other's every quirk and mood, and they relied on each other in the most vexing of circumstances. Nevertheless, for the thirty-nine years they'd worked together, Ruthie had, despite his early insistence, never once called Dr. Egan by his first name.

He wrote out the prescription. Of course she was right. He would likely have forgotten, as they both knew, his protestation mere ritual. Yet on serious matters it was Ruthie, alone among his intimates, to whom he'd never lied. To his children to spare them pain or hurt, Helen also, most memorably when she'd come so near dying early in their marriage. *The fever is subsiding, dear. Patients like you always recover.* Lies to protect himself at times, though nothing scandalous or malicious, simple selfishness or irresponsibility. And, of course, there were sometimes overly optimistic equivocations for his patients, though he tried to temper these with less sanguine possibilities.

Dr. Egan closed up, crossed the street, and went into Moore's Drug Store. At the elevated back counter, the pharmacist surveyed those below as a ship captain might view a foolish but entertaining crew. Florid-faced and corpulent, bald but for a single lock that curled atop his head, Paul Moore brought to mind the cherub on Gerber labels. As the bulging white smock revealed, the pharmacist was a man of large appetites, including a fondness for expensive brandy. He also enjoyed classical music and literature, particularly Shakespeare, which befit his Falstaffian manner.

"Another of your potions to fill, doctor, and at closing time no less?" Paul sighed. "We alchemists, unlike physicians, have little enough time already for leisurely pursuits."

"Your weight and blood pressure argue otherwise," Egan responded. "The years of carousing are catching up with you."

"Indeed," Moore admitted ruefully. "I have heard the chimes at midnight, though sadly less and less."

"Nevertheless, you are past due for a checkup, so come in on your own or I'll send Ruthie to fetch you," Egan said, and handed over the script. "This doesn't need to be filled until morning."

Dr. Egan stepped out of the drugstore. Passing Holder's Soda Shop, he told himself again that Naomi Hampton's going to Tennessee was for the best.

4

I T WAS MIDAFTERNOON when the dirt road dipped a last time and the Clarkes' mailbox appeared at the turnaround. Blackburn parked beside Mr. Clarke's pickup, in its bed four hefty Dekalb seed sacks. A creek separated the turnaround from the yard and house. Carton in hands, he crossed a small bridge and entered the yard. Naomi's father was in the field with his draft horse, the moldboard plow rippling the black soil. As Blackburn entered the yard, Mr. Clarke paused and waved, jostled the reins, and returned to work.

Two weeks ago, the day after the confrontation outside the soda shop, Naomi's father had scowled when he saw his daughter coming across this yard, Blackburn behind her bearing a travel grip and tote sack. Mr. Clarke had been contrary with Naomi, and none too friendly with him at first, but before leaving Blackburn had helped the older man chop up a yellow poplar for firewood. *You handle that ax good as a lumberjack,* he'd told Blackburn. After that he acted friendlier. They'd talked about what crops Mr. Clarke would plant come spring, what the almanac claimed the best time for each, then parted with a handshake.

As Blackburn stepped onto the porch, the door opened. Naomi's smile alone made the trip worthwhile.

"I heard a truck and was so much hoping it was you." She touched the smock where it covered her stomach. "Just look at me. I'm ripening up like a pumpkin, ain't I?"

"Naw, you look," Blackburn stammered, "well, the way you're supposed to look."

"It's a load to carry," Naomi sighed, but he heard pride in her voice as she stepped back for him to enter. "Oh Blackburn, it so lifts my heart to see you."

"I brought you a few things," he said as he stepped inside.

A fire burned in the hearth. On the fireboard was a daguerreotype of Naomi and her sister as young girls, stacked next to it a *Webster's Dictionary* and *Heath Readers,* a third book titled *Child-Life Arithmetics.* A shotgun leaned in the corner, bringing to mind Naomi's threat to Billy Runyon in January.

"Where do you want me to set this?" Blackburn asked.

"The table's fine," Naomi said.

The fire made the room warm and cozy. At the farmhouse back in Blowing Rock, Naomi had always wanted a hearth fire, claiming furnace heat didn't warm a body the way a real fire did. Blackburn suddenly felt awkward, unsure what to do. It was different at the farmhouse. There he was used to taking a seat at the kitchen table. They'd talk or play cards awhile, sometimes just sit. If Naomi needed to lie down and rest a few minutes, there was always some chore needing to be done.

"You been doing okay?" Blackburn asked.

"Lila checks on me most every day," Naomi said. "When my time gets closer, I'll stay with her, like I promised Dr. Egan I would."

"You all favored each other growing up," Blackburn said, nodding at the fireboard.

"Still do, though she's kept some weight from having her babies." Naomi lifted the wedding anniversary photograph from the carton. "Thank you so much for getting this, Blackburn."

She took more items out, a cardboard box of Dixon pencils, an Eversharp ink pen, two Blue Horse tablets, stationery, stamps. Last a wooden toy tractor.

"That one's for the baby, not you," Blackburn said, the left side of his mouth crinkling.

"It's kindly of you to bring all this," Naomi said. "Let me fetch my pocketbook."

"I ain't taking no money," Blackburn said. "It only cost a trifle, and that tractor was something I got as a young'un."

"Well, it's sweet of you," Naomi said. "Now take off that coat and hat and sit down. I'll get us some coffee."

As Naomi set the cups on the table, Blackburn took out his handkerchief and balled it into his fist. He didn't like to drink where people could watch, but Naomi was at least used to it.

"You heard from Jacob?"

"His last letter said he didn't know what cold was till he got to Korea, but claims otherwise he's fine. He's not written about any fighting. Likely wouldn't, would he, not wanting me to fret?"

"He'll be fine."

"I tell myself that," Naomi said. "Like I told him before he left, we always seem to get through the rough patches."

Blackburn took a drink of coffee, raised the handkerchief to wipe the right side of his mouth.

"Thought any more about when you'll be back?"

"I still figure end of August. I thought about staying here longer, but North Carolina's me and this baby's home, least-ways for now," Naomi answered. "I ain't wrote Jacob about what happened in Blowing Rock with his daddy, just that I come back here early, but soon as he's home safe you bet I will, and about Billy Runyon too." She paused. "The best thing for us is to move away. We should have already done it."

"Once Jacob's back things will get better," Blackburn said. "Anyway, you ought to dwell on happy notions."

"I'm trying to, especially about this baby," Naomi said, nodding toward the window. "I been watching that redbud for two weeks. There's some color on the branches so it's starting to wake up. Seeing new life sprouting all around reminds me birthing a child's a natural thing. I planted some marigolds last week too. I told myself by the time they bloom, I'll be nuzzling this baby in my arms."

They talked a while longer, before Naomi uttered a soft *oh* and placed a hand on her stomach.

"This tyke is restless today."

"Nothing's wrong?" Blackburn asked, concern in his voice.

"No, just letting me know it's there," Naomi answered, her words softening. "If you was to come and put your hand where mine is, you could feel the baby moving."

Blackburn hesitated.

"It ain't proper to ask such a thing, is it?" Naomi asked.

"It's just that no one seems to think this baby's near special as me. Lila's had three so it's not a wonder to her or Daddy either."

Blackburn's eyes were on his coffee cup. He stared at the cup a few more moments, then got up and stood beside Naomi. She placed his palm on her belly. Her hand remained on his. Through the muslin, Blackburn felt the warmth of her skin. How long since he'd touched another person? Pete Sorrells had thanked him in February after his mother's funeral. Before that, Jacob's handshake. Blackburn started to withdraw his hand.

"Wait," Naomi said.

He felt it then, a bump, soon after another one.

Then came the sound of Mr. Clarke's boots on the porch steps. The door opened but he didn't come all the way in.

"You willing to help me a minute, Blackburn?" he asked. "Got some seed sacks in my truck."

"Running a farm by yourself ain't no easy job," Mr. Clarke said as they walked to the pickup. "You got a wife or one of your children around, leastways one that ain't big with a baby, you can manage, but otherwise it'll wear you to a nub. I ought never let Naomi go to that damn hotel, even if we did need the cash money. I should have known a town boy'd catch her eye."

At the turnaround, Mr. Clarke unhitched the tailgate.

"Gonna take two trips."

"No," Blackburn said. "Just heft them on my shoulders."

Mr. Clarke looked doubtful but Blackburn managed all four.

"Where do they go?"

"The shed."

Recrossing the bridge was tricky, but the rest was easy enough. Blackburn knelt and slid the sacks off his shoulders, stacked them in a neat pile. As the men stepped out of the shed, Blackburn looked out on the fresh-plowed field. The soil had a rich, welcoming smell. Clarkes had farmed here a century, Naomi had told him, and you could tell. They'd cared for this land. Blackburn thought of his family's dream of owning a farm, how hard they'd all worked but somehow never gotten ahead enough to buy a place of their own.

"Going to grow cabbage and corn mainly this year," Mr. Clarke said, "that and my tobacco allotment. You said your daddy growed tobacco, didn't you?"

"Yes sir."

"Then you know it ain't no easy thing," Mr. Clarke said, paused. "That why your folks went to Florida, figuring picking them oranges easier?"

"Part of it, I guess."

They stared at the tilled land a few more moments. Blackburn remembered another field, him on its edge, drenched in sweat, unable to get his legs to work, his throat so constricted that he couldn't call for help.

"I best get going," he said.

"No need to rush off," Mr. Clarke said.

"It's a long drive and hard weather's coming," Blackburn answered, then went across the yard to where Naomi waited on the porch.

"I do wish you could stay longer," she told him. "We've hardly had time to talk."

"I'll be back next month to check on you," he said, glancing at the sky. "Why don't you go to your sister's house. If it was to snow bad . . ."

"I'll be fine," Naomi said.

"I won't rest easy if you don't," Blackburn said. "If need be, I'll take you."

"No, Daddy can drive me there."

"But you'll go?"

"Yes," Naomi said, "but I'll need to pack a tote first."

She'd never hugged him before but now Naomi did. Blackburn felt the press of her belly.

"Thank you so much, Blackburn, for everything. You're ever a blessing. Me and Jacob love you, and this baby will too."

As Blackburn drove back to North Carolina, his thoughts turned to Billy Runyon. It had started in the sixth grade, Billy's bullying, the nicknames, the trips and shoves. Billy was no bigger than Blackburn, just meaner, and had friends like Troy Williamson to back him up. After that school year, Blackburn's parents needed him for farm work. A blessing, but there were still times Blackburn saw Billy in town. If no adults were looking, a taunt, in his early teens an arm punch with it. But when Billy quit growing, Blackburn didn't, and grave digging work built more muscles than pumping gas and cleaning windshields. Billy kept his distance, Blackburn like a dog on a chain that had held years but might yet snap.

But on Halloween night two years ago, Blackburn heard a car outside, its headlights aimed at the cottage. *Come on out here, Blackburn, these gals want to see you,* Billy yelled. A girl in the car shrieked as Billy tried to pull her from the backseat. They finally left, but not before bottles and cans were tossed from the windows, gravel scattered as the car veered back down the drive. Then in January, Billy and Troy showed up at the farmhouse drunk, something they'd never have dared with Jacob there. He remembered Billy's smirk when Naomi came out on the porch with the rifle, and how quickly that smirk vanished when Naomi pulled the trigger.

Blackburn made good time. The road between Pulaski and Knoxville was mainly level, few curves. Before driving Naomi to her father's house two weeks ago, Blackburn had never seen land that looked flattened by a rolling pin, streams dark and slow as molasses. Without hills or mountains, no crops yet rising in the fields, the land's openness exposed too much. Though it was dark now, as he passed Knoxville Blackburn felt relief as the headlights tilted upward.

As he crossed the state line, flakes of snow began to fall. By the time he got to Laurel Fork, the road was white. He passed Hampton's Store. The Gulf sign, frozen to its hinges, no longer swayed. Even the gas pumps seemed hunched against the cold. Once back at the cemetery, Blackburn found a note taped to the cottage door.

Mindy Timberlake died today. Funeral Thursday so need the grave dug Wednesday. Let me know if you want me to call Neil Wease. Also, need light switch replaced in back hallway.

Reverend H.

The wind picked up, and a gust swept snow sideways. The belfry bell clanged once, stilled. Blackburn went into the church. In the foyer, he dusted snow off his hat and coat, hung them on a peg. He switched on the lights, checked the furnace before turning the bathroom faucets enough to drip and keep the pipes from freezing. That done, Blackburn walked down the side aisle and sat in the pew nearest the church's single stained-glass window. Its corners were like patches on a quilt—orange, green, yellow, blue. In the center a gentle-faced angel, its white wings open as if to embrace Blackburn. On sunny afternoons when the light slanted in, the window glowed. The colored light would wash over Blackburn and he'd briefly feel that the world, himself included, was something more than it appeared. He hadn't prayed much since childhood, but he did now. *Yes,* Blackburn whispered, *leave here and go protect them.* He walked back up the aisle. As he switched off one sanctuary light, then the second, the angel slowly receded.

5

JACOB AWOKE TO WHISPERS OVERHEAD. The North Koreans had found him, perhaps seen a blood trail leading to the cutbank. Whispers again, softer this time though, farther downriver. Then silence. The pain in his shoulder flared as Jacob inched forward. His head emerged. Cold and windy, but the sun was out. Already midmorning. He could see the opposite shore, a line of stark trees above the sand. No sentry. Lieutenant Pike said they'd be moving today, back the way they'd come, and by now they'd have given him up for dead. Jacob waited to let the North Koreans get farther away. He listened awhile longer in case some had stayed behind.

Last night while he was on guard duty, the river looked so narrow, so easily crossed. Now it seemed wide as a reservoir. He saw the knife blade jutting out of the ice and, closer to the opposite bank, his rifle, dusted white. Enough snow to cover what blood had been spilled. Jacob pondered what a soldier on shore would think. Most likely study where the ice had buckled and assume both men had drowned. They'd see the knife blade, but wouldn't want to dwell on that.

Sunlight fell on the river, not only brightening the ice but warming it. *Like a blind man on a ledge,* Jacob thought as he set his right hand onto the surface, then his knees. He paused. The enemy soldiers weren't far away. One glance back at the river and they might see him, but each moment the ice warmed a little more. Lost blood, the cold, he'd not survive another night. *You ain't got a choice,* he told himself. Jacob crawled farther out, left arm dragging at his side, limp fingers furrowing the light snow. All the while listening for the click of a safety. But no shot came. Perhaps he was so mud-daubed that he looked more animal than human.

By the time he neared mid-river, his right hand was numb. Jacob stopped, rose to his knees. He placed the hand under his clothing, palm pressed against his belly, to get some feeling back. Here the sun was at its brightest. For a few moments, Jacob closed his eyes, face upward, seeking its warmth. If the North Koreans saw him now, would they think he was beseeching God while awaiting execution?

Jacob moved forward and felt a skim of water. He could see the river's darkness under the ice. He reached his hand out, set it down. As Jacob shifted his knees, a crackle. He slid his hand back slowly, as if to soothe the ice. Which would the morning sun's angle warm first, upstream or down? It should have been easy to figure out, but even when Jacob confirmed the slant, it took moments to clear his mind, turn and face downstream. His hand was completely numb, each forward placement confirmed by eyesight as much as feel. How much farther downstream? An idea came that he could follow the river all the way to the ocean. But that was fatigue and cold muddling his mind. He crawled a few more yards, turned toward the shore. This time the ice held. He did not look up until he touched sand. He staggered up the bank and found last night's encampment abandoned.

Two days ago, villagers had greeted the unit warmly, even warned Mullins, who knew some Korean, that the enemy was across the river. It had been there that Jacob had given the child a pack of chewing gum, the child's father two cigarettes. He followed the path to the village. At his approach, men and women cowered. Others waved Jacob away with arm gestures.

The child recognized him first, then the father.

"*Gwisin*," a villager said, gesturing for Jacob not to come nearer.

Jacob raked mud off his uniform and hair and face.

"No, American, GI."

"*Gwisin*," the villager said.

Then Jacob understood. He opened his right hand and slapped it against his arm and then his chest.

"See, alive."

When the villagers remained unconvinced, Jacob took the bayonet from the scabbard, slid the blade across the thumb of his left hand. Not deep, but enough to draw blood.

The father nodded for Jacob to follow him to a thatch hut at the rear of the village. He motioned for Jacob to sit on a bed of knitted sheaves and started a fire. Soapy water was brought in a tin bucket. The man helped Jacob strip to his waist and began cleaning the wounds with a washcloth. As the man dipped the cloth in the bucket, the water inside reddened. Jacob felt a new fear. In this climate, cold sometimes cauterized a soldier's wounds. Still alive, able to talk, but the medics knew once their bodies warmed that the bleeding would resume. But as the depth of the slashes on his shoulder and side became visible, Jacob was reassured. The villager placed the cloth in the bucket, helped him get his clothing back on as the boy set a water canister and a wooden bowl at the hut's center. Jacob drank, then scooped up the food. The father and son watched.

Afterward, Jacob lay on the matting. The man placed a bright patched quilt over him and left. The last of the cold began to leave his body. As the afternoon waned, two men helped Jacob onto an oxcart, heaped hay over him, and set out. Each time the cart jolted, the pain in his arm and shoulder flared, but after a while the path widened and smoothed. Jacob thought again of the night he and Naomi met, how quickly he'd felt so much.

Infatuation, his mother called it. His father had said the same, adding that Jacob was merely trying to vex them. If it were true, they'd deserved it. Jacob had been so tired of his parents deciding every aspect of his life. Sending him to Blowing Rock's schools, telling him how to speak, whom to be friends with and date, nagging him into college and, even after a summer proving himself at the sawmill, trying to make him re-enroll. And marrying Naomi, wanting to decide that too, as if being unable to shape his sisters' lives gave his parents the *right* to make Jacob into exactly what they wanted.

Jacob remembered the day after he and Naomi moved into the farmhouse, his parents showing up with Lawyer Bennett. *If you refuse an annulment, we'll change our will so you inherit nothing. But if you get the annulment now, in two years you and Naomi can still marry, with our blessing. It will be for the best, for her and you.*

If he were honest, there were times Jacob feared his parents might be right. Not embarrassed but nevertheless aware when Naomi said or did something that caused people in town to smirk. There had been a few quarrels, as with all couples. Then all was fine again. Yet his parents had placed just enough doubt inside him that it lingered like an infection. Until, that was, last night on the river. Beneath the moon's brightness, the sole truth of what mattered had been revealed.

The cart paused a few moments and Jacob tensed. Voices, but the words exchanged had no stridency. The cart went on. For the first time since the fight on the ice, Jacob knew he would survive.

6

ON WEDNESDAY MORNING, the snow had stopped
but the thermometer read twenty-five degrees. Beneath the white, the earth would be like iron. Wilkie
had warned Blackburn that in winter there'd be days like this,
so left Blackburn playing cards and a closet shelf stacked with
Zane Grey novels. The pages were brittle as dry leaves, some
fallen out and lost. Silverfish-gnawed, mildewed, though that
didn't matter. A cowboy got into a bad fix and then got out of
it, so what happened was easy enough to fill in. Wilkie also left
jigsaw puzzles, pieces missing, but like the paperbacks, once
finished everything was clear enough. In January, Blackburn
had bought a new puzzle at Moore's Drug Store, a thousand-
piece Falcon de luxe he and Naomi spent an afternoon putting together.

As Blackburn played solitaire, the temperature rose. Sunlight softened the snow and by late morning he could get the
truck down the drive. On Laurel Fork Road he met no other
vehicles, saw no people outside, the creek itself a dark thread

amid the whiteness. Until he entered Blowing Rock, it was as if the cemetery's stillness had spread over the whole world.

Blackburn parked and crossed the street to Weaver's Hardware. *Never let Naomi go in there,* Jacob had warned. Before, Blackburn had liked the store's weathered oak-planked floor, the familiar odor of linseed oil and feed. Everything had its proper place—shovels, mattocks, axes, and rakes lined up against the back wall, nails and fence staples on the opposite aisle. Nothing frivolous. Even the light was just enough, two dusty bulbs leaving the corners shadowy. But in January when Blackburn set curtain rods and a kitchen faucet on the counter, Mr. Weaver had glared at him, which was no surprise since the Weavers, like most people in town, had expected Jacob and Veronica to marry one day.

Blackburn kicked snow off his boots and went inside to buy the switch kit. Mr. Weaver was with a customer so Veronica stood at the counter.

"For the church," Blackburn told her.

Before ringing up the purchase, Veronica looked to see where her father was, then asked if Blackburn or the Hamptons had heard from Jacob.

"I hope he's safe," she said when Blackburn shook his head that he hadn't. "Some folks might doubt me, but I wish Jacob well, his wife and that coming child the same."

Once outside, Blackburn looked up the sidewalk at the Yonahlossee, cursed others, himself.

The theater wasn't crowded and he'd guided her to an empty side row. When the picture ended and the houselights came on, he motioned for Naomi to stay seated. Even so, they were noticed—a glare, a headshake, muttered words. Once the theater emptied, they walked under the red EXIT sign onto the sidewalk.

Naomi nodded toward Holder's Soda Shop.

I'd sure love some hot chocolate, Naomi said. Okay?

He stepped to the shop window and peered in. No one but the soda jerk, but before Blackburn opened the glass door for Naomi, he saw Mark Lutz standing outside his shoe store, looking their way.

All right, but we need to get it to go.

In the shop, a radio played a song about a Chattanooga shoe-shine boy. The soda jerk was washing bowls and ignored them until Blackburn finally tapped a quarter on the Formica counter and ordered. Yeah, I'm coming, the man snapped, but took his time. Twenty-six cents, he said, placing the cup on the counter. He swept the coins into his hand dismissively and turned away.

Blackburn was about to ask for a lid when the red Oldsmobile pulled into a parking space across the street.

We need to go, Blackburn said.

As he and Naomi walked down the sidewalk, Mr. Hampton crossed the street and stood between them and Jacob's truck.

It's not enough you being with a man alone in my son's house, is it, you hussy? Hampton seethed. No, got to humiliate our family in front of the whole town.

We're leaving now, Blackburn said, but Hampton didn't move.

As soon as Jacob's back home, me and him are leaving here, Naomi answered, her voice harsh as Hampton's. You'll never see Jacob again. Nor his baby.

Bystanders crowded closer and Hampton turned his fury on them.

Go ahead and gawk, you damn busybodies. I know what you've been saying behind our backs about her and us. You don't say it to our faces though, do you? Or when you need credit at the store or a place to rent or work.

Sheriff Triplett pushed through the onlookers.

What's this about, Mr. Hampton?

Look at her, damn it. Parading that big belly around, making sure everyone sees it. Fancied up like a harlot. And look at Gant here, if your eyes can stand it. He claims to be Jacob's friend. My son's in Korea because of her, Triplett, and I'll damn well have my say.

He has every right, someone shouted from the crowd now spilling onto the street.

Please, Mr. Hampton, Sheriff Triplett said. Let's not make this any worse.

It can't be any worse, the older man answered, but let himself be ushered to the side. Blackburn took her hand and tried to push through the crowd, but Naomi was jostled and fell to the curb. As Blackburn knelt beside her, Dr. Egan made his way through the onlookers.

You get these people back, Sheriff, Egan demanded as he too knelt beside Naomi. Don't you know what something like this could do?

I hope she does have a miscarriage, Egan, Hampton said. That would be the best thing for all of us.

Come afternoon as Blackburn opened the cemetery gate, sun struck the snow with a daunting brightness. Because smaller markers lay beneath the white leveling, the cemetery appeared emptier, as if making room for newer occupants. A portent, Wilkie would doubtless have thought. *Don't let your mind dwell on such things,* Blackburn told himself, but as he stared at the cemetery, he remembered lying limb-weak and sweating beside the tobacco field. Now, as then, came a fear that something he'd be unable to stop was beginning.

Equipment gathered and placed, Blackburn started digging. At first, the ground was so hard he had to pry the mattock blade free. Chunks of dirt hit the tarp like chert rock. But soon the ground softened. As he scooped another shovelful, something sparked in the sunlight. Wilkie once found an 1898 silver dollar and claimed a grave digger near Morganton had unearthed a Spanish doubloon, but this was just a mica shard. Blackburn had found coins, but they were usually on the graves' surfaces and purposely placed there, not lost. And not only coins but thimbles, fish lures, hairpins, pocketknives.

Wilkie had left behind a book called *Funeral Customs: Their Origin and Development,* which described objects placed on or in graves for use in the afterlife. Zulus and Greeks were buried with jewelry and spears. Romans interred coins as payment for passage. When Blackburn asked Wilkie if such things as thimbles and knives were there for similar reasons, the old man considered the question carefully. *There's needs a-plenty in this world and maybe in the next one too.* For whatever reason, unlike flowers and wreaths, such offerings were made discreetly. Suddenly there, as if dropped from the sky.

Blackburn, like his predecessor, let them stay. As months passed, they slowly sank from sight.

The sun held steady in the sky. By late afternoon, hidden gravestones emerged. Outside the cemetery, ice sleeves slipped off limbs, a brittle chiming as they shattered. Blackburn's boots and overalls were lathered in mud. Soon the grave's depth required him to lower the stepladder and enter. Wilkie said his greatest fear was being trapped in a grave overnight, that he'd dreamed about it constantly. Sometimes Blackburn had the same dream and suspected all grave diggers did. Now, though awake, Blackburn also felt a familiar foreboding that the grave floor might give like a scaffold's trapdoor, send him hurtling into darkness. He lifted his feet off the bottom rung one at a time.

After another hour, Blackburn began to tire. When he first took the caretaker's job, Reverend Hunnicutt paid Neil Wease or Buck Murdock three dollars to help. Wease didn't mind dropping a cigarette butt in the grave or cursing when his mattock hit a root or rock. He'd sing dirty songs and sip from a flask holstered in his back pocket. Though no more than five-six, if Wease was in the grave and couldn't see the surface, he declared it deep enough. *They'll get out quicker come resurrection day,* Wease would joke as he tossed up his shovel and climbed out. Blackburn would finish the job. Murdock, who'd spent five years in prison, was quieter but chewed tobacco and spit. Unless it was bitterly cold, Murdock wore no shirt. After a few months, Blackburn told Reverend Hunnicutt he preferred to work alone.

Daylight waned as Blackburn pitched the shovel on the snow and climbed the ladder. He placed the second tarp over the earth he'd dug, took his tools to the shed. Coming back, he paused and looked across the road at the Hamptons' pasture. Jacob's parents had planned to build Jacob a house there, but that was before he and Naomi eloped. Blackburn remembered when Jacob brought Naomi to the cemetery. She was barely up to Jacob's shoulder. So young-looking, yet Blackburn saw why Jacob was smitten. Naomi had a special kind of prettiness—blue eyes but hair shiny black as fresh-broke coal. What Blackburn remembered most though was her white-and-brown saddles, their leather worn, some eyelets missing. The shoestrings were new though, their bright whiteness doubtless to make the shoes look nicer. Naomi's doing so had moved Blackburn in a way he had no word for, then or now. He thought about her beside him at the picture show. Whether soap or perfume, a scent like honeysuckle lingered on her skin. During moments of silence, Blackburn heard her breathing, the touch of Naomi's hand on his arm when something on the screen surprised her.

He went around the cottage to the back porch, stripped to his union suit, and scrubbed the dirt off with a pail of water and Lava soap. He put on clean clothes and lit the wood stove's kindling. Beans were in the kettle and corn bread in the warming closet. There was buttermilk in the springhouse but Blackburn warmed up coffee instead. He placed firewood on the andirons, kindling beneath, and struck the match. Flames wove around the logs like vines.

"Catch," he told the fire. Other than the three he'd said to Veronica Weaver at the store, it was the first word he'd spoken in two days.

The cemetery's seeming emptiness earlier still troubled

Blackburn. His thoughts turned to Jacob. In Korea, a new day had hardly begun. Even colder there, more dangerous. *It was just snow covering up some grave markers, nothing more,* Blackburn told himself, yet when he closed his eyes, he still saw white gaps amid the stones.

7

WHEN THE TELETYPE CHATTERED and Ben Parson saw NAOMI HAMPTON BLOWING ROCK NORTH CAROLINA THE SECRETARY OF THE ARMY REGRETS, he turned away as the tape continued to roll. He had delivered too many of these telegrams during World War II, enough that when families saw his truck coming they averted their eyes, as if acknowledgment could provoke death to look their way. Some residents crossed the street to avoid him. Six such telegrams during World War II, all but one announcing a death. They'd had a right to fear him. After the war ended, people met his eyes again. But now there was fighting in Korea. Three boys were already over there, Ryan Calhoun, James Story, and Jacob Hampton. More would be going, possibly Eric, his own son, who'd be eligible in another year. The last of the tape came and the teletype stilled.

Daniel Hampton had been right. The girl was beyond shameless. Parson had witnessed it himself, her stout with child and in public with a man not her husband, watching a picture show together at the Yonahlossee and after that on to

Holder's Soda Shop. Such an affront to the whole community made Parson wonder if rumors about the child's paternity were true. Gossips in town took pleasure in the scandal, as did others who thought the Hamptons high-nosed and over-bearing, but what Daniel had claimed on the sidewalk that afternoon was true. The Hamptons had helped many people survive the Depression, including Parson's own family. Cora had given his parents credit at their store and never charged interest, never once threatened to cut them off. They'd done the same for many others, including old folks who would never pay back their debt. While other businesses laid off em-ployees, Daniel had made certain every man at the sawmill got a few hours of work each week. *Bad times hone people to their core,* Parson's mother had said, and, whatever else they were, at the Hamptons' core was hard work and decency.

The tape lay coiled like a snake readying to strike. Two of Cora and Daniel's children were already in Laurel Fork Cem-etery. Now, if a *third*. The office closed in fifteen minutes, excuse enough not to forward the telegram, but to show the Hamptons the message first was a federal crime. Neverthe-less, wouldn't a worse crime be having the girl know before Jacob's parents?

Get it over with, Parson told himself. He lifted the tape, read, and sighed in relief. Seriously injured, but alive. He read the tape again. If it were his son, wouldn't this be good news? Yes, Parson thought, surely so for parents who'd known far worse. He transferred the tape onto the telegram, then typed out what needed to be on the envelope, including Naomi Hampton's Tennessee address. But he did not seal it.

He locked the office and drove to Laurel Fork. Good news,

Parson thought, but as he parked in front of the store, he hesitated. It was possible the Hamptons might not see it that way. The telegram did say *seriously* injured. Mounting the steps, Parson did not speak to the old men on the porch, offered instead a sober, tight-lipped nod. Taking off his cap, he went inside. Cora was behind the counter, placing coins in a paper roll. He waited until she'd finished and stepped closer. She saw the telegram and her shoulders tensed, pulled inward.

"I'm not supposed to do this," Parson said, pointing to the Tennessee address, "but I felt you deserved to see it first."

"I knew, I knew, I knew," Cora said, each time the words softer, more hollow. Her right hand reached out and grasped the counter.

He'd seen this before, everything in a person: face, shoulders, even voice, *collapsing*.

"Cora," Parson said, the only time he'd ever called her by her first name. He hesitated, then spoke. "Jacob's alive. Read it. You'll see."

But she seemed not to believe him, even as he set the telegram on the counter.

"No," Cora said, her hand trembling. "I want Daniel to be here."

Parson turned and stepped away as she lifted the phone's bell to her ear and dialed. After speaking a few words into the mouthpiece, she placed the bell back on the hook.

When Daniel arrived, he saw the telegram and his face paled. He went around the counter and stood beside Cora. Neither reached to open it.

"I'll be on the porch," Parson said, but not before offering a reassuring nod.

When he stepped outside, the old men were gone, except for Joel Matney, a Great War veteran, who stood like a sentinel next to the gas pumps, ensuring no one entered the store. The town would soon know Parson had delivered the telegram to the Hamptons, and if a few people, even one, realized what he'd done . . . *I should have brought it to their house, in the dark.* But it was too late for that. Parson looked across the road. Uphill, the church spire daggered the sky. How long before another army telegram came—days, months, a year, possibly about his own son? World War II had ended just six years ago. Hadn't the country done enough fighting, had enough boys killed, without leaping headlong into another one?

The store's door finally opened.

"You've done us a kindness, Ben," Cora said, again joining Daniel behind the counter.

"I have to send it on in the morning," Parson said.

"We understand," Cora said.

"We'll need to keep it until then," Daniel said. "I'm going to make a phone call or two and may need the information."

"I don't think . . ."

"Just until morning," Daniel said firmly. "I'll bring it to you first thing tomorrow."

Parson hesitated.

"All right," he answered reluctantly.

As he drove home, Parson thought of the scene weeks ago in town, the girl's inappropriate dress and garish makeup. Done deliberately too, he was sure of that. He thought about the Hamptons' relief when she'd left for Tennessee the following day. Nevertheless, if the hussy's threat was true, Jacob would move away and never return. Wouldn't that be almost as bad as losing a son to death? Maybe things would somehow work out between Jacob and his parents. *I did the right thing*, he told himself, but Parson could not quell the sense that he had opened himself up to a world of trouble.

8

D ESPITE PARSON'S ASSURANCE TO CORA, as Daniel
had stared at the telegram, its thin paper seemed
more solid than the counter, the shelves, the store
itself. *At this moment my son is alive,* he'd told himself. *Only if
I withdraw the contents of this envelope can it be otherwise.* An
irrational thought, but Cora did not touch the telegram either. Daniel's mind had reeled backward. After burying their
daughters, he and Cora tried to have another child. A year
passed before consulting Egan. Following the doctor's ad-
vice, they'd checked the calendar for the most fertile times,
even used a thermometer. The humiliation of that when the
poorest sharecropper could fill a shack with a dozen children. Seven more years, then, when they'd all but given up,
Cora became pregnant. Daniel remembered Jacob's premature birth, how terrified he and Cora were. Such a precari-
ous beginning. They'd kept him out of the county swimming
pool because of polio. Every sneeze or cough meant a trip
to Dr. Egan. Overprotective, but how not to be after twice

learning how fragile children's lives were. And yet not protective enough . . . Daniel remembered Cora's raised hand in December, her vow. *I will not endure it.*

At the store, Cora had been the one who took out the telegram, set it before them so they could read at the same time.

THE SECRETARY OF THE ARMY EXPRESSES HIS DEEP REGRET THAT YOUR HUSBAND PVT HAMPTON JACOB W HAS BEEN SERIOUSLY INJURED IN KOREA SINCE 18 MAR 51 AS RESULT OF HYPOTHERMIA COMMA WOUNDS SIDE OF NECK COMMA LEFT SHOULDER COMMA RIB CAGE COMMA INCURRED IN COMBAT STOP MAIL MAY BE FORWARDED TO HIM QUOTE RANK NAME SERVICE NUMBER C/O HOSPITAL DIRECTORY SECTION APO 503 C/O POSTMASTER SAN FRANCISCO CALIFORNIA

After Parson had left, they'd locked up the store and gone to the house. Daniel called the army recruitment office and Sergeant Ross, whose son worked at the sawmill, promised to find out more about Jacob. He called back an hour later. Ross couldn't get through to the overseas hospital directly, but he'd found someone who could: surgery on Jacob's shoulder but no limb lost, frostbite treated. *He'll be home by summer and a hero to boot,* Ross told Daniel. *Your boy's likely to be nominated for a Bronze Star.*

Now, the dishes washed and put up, the telegram lay before them on the kitchen table. They'd always had their most important conversations here—after the loss of their daughters, after Jacob's elopement. The parlor felt too open, the dining room and its table too wide. The kitchen was intimate, a small space nestled deep inside the house. The room's drop table was so small his and Cora's feet often touched. Intimate and unchanged—the same porcelain salt and pepper shakers and sugar bowl, same blue-and-white Vinylite mat. The relief they felt earlier was muted.

"If only this could be the blessing for us, for our family, that it should be," Cora said. "People say things always happen for a reason. For once, I want to believe it's true . . . that, somehow, this could truly bring Jacob back to us."

Daniel waited. She had always been smarter, quicker. Cora could add up most purchases without need of the register, do the books at the store and sawmill in half the time it took him. But numbers weren't all she could solve. In the early months after Black Tuesday, she'd been the one who realized that, despite the rail costs, selling the sawmill's lumber directly to buyers in Atlanta and Charlotte could keep them afloat.

There were people in the county who'd have been pleased to see the Hamptons humbled, the store and sawmill lost to the bank, their eighty acres auctioned off. In 1931 it almost happened, their savings depleted, store and sawmill mortgaged. Cora had saved them then also. As other businesses in and around Blowing Rock closed, she filled Hampton's Store and back porch with the liquidated stock of former competitors: yellowware, lanterns and brogans, combs and cookware, mops and brooms. She'd bartered for galax and ginseng, avoided middlemen to double the profit. By 1933 they had enough money to buy fifty more acres and two houses in Blowing Rock to turn into rentals. The same people in the community who'd hoped they'd go bankrupt now begged for store credit and work at the sawmill.

They'd done it for Jacob. When other children lacked shoes, slept in rooms where snow blew through board gaps, he never once knew want. Always provided for, kept from harm. Had he agreed to the annulment and stayed in college, Jacob would be in a classroom, not an army hospital. And they'd still be a family, the girl back in Tennessee, forgotten, perhaps Jacob and Veronica Weaver engaged.

"There must be something we can do," Cora said.

"We could give her money," Daniel suggested, "like we talked about in January."

"I still don't think she'd take it," Cora answered. "Even if she did, Jacob would go after her, if for no other reason than the child."

"It's like that damn hussy bewitched him," Daniel said. "The things I said to her, to him, I know I shouldn't have, but still . . ."

"No good to dwell on the past," Cora said.

Nevertheless, that night in bed, Daniel did ponder the past. His father had doled out punishment with a strap. They'd go to the woodshed, where Daniel was forced to bare his buttocks and place his hands on the wall. *I will teach you to obey, boy,* his father would tell him. The whippings left red welts that, as the days passed, deepened to purple. Daniel yet bore marks from those whippings. He'd vowed never to do such a thing to his own children and kept that vow. Daniel remembered a morning when, after warnings never to cross the road alone, Jacob had anyway. He'd almost been hit by a truck. Daniel and Cora had been so frightened they'd done nothing except hug the boy. How old was Jacob then, four, maybe five? Young, but Daniel knew what his father would have done: a lesson in obedience, one that would never be forgotten.

Later, when Jacob was a teenager, he and Cora tried to reason with him, even compromising about college. Try it one year, they'd said, believing once there he'd stay all four, marry Veronica Weaver, and begin taking over the family business. But when May arrived, Jacob had announced he wouldn't go back to school but instead work at the sawmill. *We'll let him,* Daniel told Cora, thinking a few months under a summer sun would change Jacob's mind. He'd put Jacob to work as a stacker, the hardest job at the sawmill, and told Bo Higgins to make Jacob more than ready to sit in a classroom come September. The foreman rode the boy hard, but Jacob didn't shirk or complain. By midsummer Higgins said Jacob was the best stacker in the yard. Nevertheless, he and Cora still believed come September he'd listen to them and return to school.

Then the Clarke girl ruined it all. *I will not endure it,* Cora had said last December, then raised an open hand toward the cemetery, toward Daniel too. No matter what had come at them in their three decades of marriage, Cora had never surrendered. She had always found a way to enable them to go on, but that December morning she'd finally been broken.

Yes, Daniel thought, if he could go back to that long-ago afternoon when Jacob wandered into the road, there would be no hugs. He would drag him into the woodshed, take off his belt, and flay the boy's buttocks till they bled.

. . .

Come morning when Daniel awoke, Cora was already in the kitchen. Not sipping coffee, just sitting, thumb pressed against her index finger. As if to pull a thread that might unravel an answer. He'd seen the same gesture those early nights of the Depression. Daniel suspected Cora had been up for hours. When he sat down, she met his eyes.

"I think I know what can be done, not everything but most of it. Parson has to be involved or else it won't work."

"Tell me."

When she was almost through, Cora looked out the window and shook her head.

"It's terrible, isn't it, to have conceived such a thing, much less believe we could do it?"

"What's terrible is having buried two children, Cora," Daniel answered, "then, despite all that's happened, knowing we could still lose the third."

"I know," Cora said. "But it should never have come to this."

"That's not our fault," Daniel said. "Whatever happens, we can't forget Jacob forced it upon us."

She explained more. Several times Daniel thought he'd found a flaw, but Cora had anticipated the problem. She explained details he hadn't thought of—having a signed contract made up, what the grave marker would say. When Daniel objected to the girl's grave being in the Hampton plot, Cora explained that Jacob would see it as an act of reconciliation.

"It could work, especially her being that far away," Daniel

said when she'd finished. "But with so many things to think about that might go wrong . . ."

"We can't decide in a couple of hours," Cora said. "We'll have to convince Parson to hold off sending the telegram, at least for a day."

"Parson saw the way that girl was behaving," Daniel said. "He knows we're in the right. And he's one of the few people around here with a sense of gratitude."

"But to convince him to then do the second part," Cora said. "We may need more than gratitude."

"If so, we've got money enough," Daniel said. "It's not yet seven thirty. He'll likely still be at home."

"Call him then, but only about the delay."

Daniel went into the front room and phoned Parson, who protested at first then sullenly agreed. As he and Cora talked more, new problems arose, new risks. In the early afternoon, Sergeant Ross called. Jacob was still confined to bed and on morphine, but he continued to improve.

"If you need anything else, you let me know, Mr. Hampton," Ross told him.

He and Cora talked until midnight.

"All it will take is one person besides Parson finding out," Cora cautioned him as they lay in bed. "But their farm sounds so isolated they don't see many people." She paused. "If Parson helps us, and the girl's father keeps his word, it could work."

Cora reached out her hands, clasped his. Not for the first time, Daniel was surprised at how small they were. She nudged closer and spoke.

"When Parson laid the telegram on the counter, I looked

down at the floor. The wood was duller from the wear of my shoes. But that was the only difference. *Thirty-two years,* I thought, *thirty-two years standing here growing old and all I have to show for it is three children taken from me.*"

"Cora . . ."

"Our life, Daniel. It's always been about trying to keep something from being taken away, hasn't it?"

"Yes, which is why we're owed so much, including our share of good luck."

"Even if it all works, it will hurt Jacob."

"At first," Daniel acknowledged, "but if not Veronica, he'll soon find someone else. We'll build the house for him in the pasture, a fine big house, the way we always planned to, and soon enough there will be children to help fill it."

"It still depends on Parson," Cora said. "The money might not be enough. Remind him he's broken some serious laws already, and if word got out . . ."

"I don't think it will come to threats."

"We'll see," Cora said.

{ II }

9

EASTER CAME EARLY THIS YEAR, only days away. By Sunday evening the cemetery would display more color than any other time. Amid the carnations and roses, some plastic, some real, ribbons and bows would add their own brightness. In preparation, Blackburn brought a trowel and bristle brush, rags and a pail of water. He began on the far back row, where white oak branches rose above the graves. Here moss and lichen grew fastest. Bleach was too harsh, Wilkie had taught him, especially for soapstone and marble. Only water should be used, and not town water either. *Got chemicals in it,* the old man claimed.

It would be a good day for such work, sunny and mild. After last week's snow, spring seemed ready to settle in. The first stone belonged to Paul Chasen, who'd killed himself in 1922. Burying suicides farthest from the church was, rightly to Blackburn, no longer done. Wasn't a life brutal enough to prefer death punishment enough? After scraping off moss and dirt with the trowel, Blackburn dipped the brush into the pail, brought it up dripping. He scrubbed the stone front and back, used a rag and forefinger to probe the chiseled indentions. Blackburn moved slowly up the row. *Shay Leary, Cal Triplett, Paul and Allie Higgins, Thomas and Sarah Matney.*

He came to Elizabeth Reed's stone, *1943–1949* carved below the name. In fourth grade, Blackburn's classmate Sally Washburn had disappeared for two months. No one knew why until Sally returned. Thick black shoes covered her feet. Leather straps cinched metal braces to her legs. Sally moved in short, wary steps, sometimes needing crutches. *Polio.* The word teachers and parents whispered, the children too, as if saying it aloud might cause what had happened to Sally to happen to them. Blackburn remembered the day beside the tobacco field when his own legs weakened. As he lay there, Blackburn had thought of Sally but even more of children he'd seen in photographs. Rows of children, all but their heads enclosed in metal tubes. And he'd thought of still others, like Elizabeth Reed, who'd been placed not inside tubes but inside coffins.

When the water gave out, Blackburn took the pail to the springhouse. He set it beneath the outflow pipe, took crumbles of corn bread from a tobacco pouch, and went in. No light but what came from the doorway. Shelves on the left held mason jars of canned vegetables, on the top row, smaller jars of sourwood honey and blackberry jam. A concrete trough ran along the opposite wall, a foot deep and two feet wide. At the far end, quart jars of milk and buttermilk. Blackburn could not see the trout. He dropped bits of corn bread and the water swirled. In the summer, he'd sit on the trough's concrete corner during work breaks. Sometimes after he sprinkled the crumbs, he'd place his hand in the water, feel the trout brush against it. As he did now, feeling what he could not see.

Blackburn thought about the rest of the day. Once the stones were cleaned, he'd drive to the farmhouse, use rope and an old tire to make a child's swing. That done, he'd ready Naomi's vegetable garden for planting, make another bed for the marigold seeds he'd bought. If he got back here in time, maybe enjoy a walk down to the Ledfords' abandoned homeplace.

He'd just returned to scrubbing when Mr. Hampton's Oldsmobile appeared. He parked and walked past the gate to the cemetery's center. Blackburn set the bristle brush beside the pail and stood. *Come to check on his daughters' graves,* he thought. Seconds passed and Blackburn grew uneasy. Jacob's father wasn't staring at his daughters' graves but at the ground beside them.

Mr. Hampton looked up, motioned Blackburn to join him.

"We've had a death and I'm going to need you to dig the grave."

Blackburn studied the older man's face. Serious, grim too, but what he didn't see was grief. Surely Jacob's great-aunt in Asheville, or the aunt in Charlotte. Nevertheless, his heart quickened. *It can't be,* Blackburn told himself. For a few moments neither spoke.

"It ain't Jacob," Blackburn said, mustering a tone of near defiance.

"No, not Jacob," Mr. Hampton said, though his face remained grim. "He's been wounded but he's going to be okay."

"He got wounded?" Blackburn stammered. "When? How?"

"The telegram didn't tell us, but he's recovering. They say he'll be home by June."

"But he'll be fine. You swear that's so," Blackburn said. "This ain't got nothing to do with Jacob. That's what you're saying, right?" He tried to meet Mr. Hampton's eyes for confirmation, but the older man stared at the space beside his daughters' stones. "Tell me it's so," Blackburn demanded.

Mr. Hampton spoke Naomi's name.

"What about her?" Blackburn said, voice quickening. "This ain't making no sense to me."

"She is why I am here," Mr. Hampton said. "Her father contacted us last night."

"Contacted you about what?" Blackburn demanded.

"About her," the older man answered, still not meeting Blackburn's eyes. "She died of a miscarriage."

"Naomi?" Blackburn said, shaking his head. "That ain't possible. I seen her last week. It's some kind of mix-up is all."

"No, Gant. It's not a mistake. She died, the baby too."

Blackburn remembered his hand pressed to Naomi's belly, the soft bump against his palm.

"I seen her," Blackburn said. "She was fine."

"Miscarriages happen suddenly," Mr. Hampton said, his somberness giving away to impatience. "There's no mistake."

"They ain't no cause for it," Blackburn said, but even as he spoke he realized there could be. "The telegram, she got one too . . . That's what you're claiming, her hearing Jacob was hurt bad . . ."

"All her father told me was that they didn't reach the hospital in time," Mr. Hampton answered. "He wants her buried here, likely doesn't want the bother or expense of doing it himself. Mrs. Hampton and I are willing to see she has a proper burial. That's all you need to know."

Too much was coming too fast to hold level. The cemetery tilted, as if all might slide off the hill, gravestones breaking free and crashing onto the road, caskets jolting open. Blackburn clenched his fist, locked his eyes on the ground.

"Are you understanding me?"

Mr. Hampton's voice sounded distant. Blackburn kept staring at the ground, at his boots. The ground leveled.

"It still could be some kind of mistake," Blackburn said more softly, looking up.

"It's not a mistake, Gant."

Silent moments passed. The words solidified inside Blackburn like stone.

"Jacob," he finally managed to say, "does he know?"

"That's not your concern. Your business is to get her buried, and it needs to be done by tomorrow morning." Mr. Hampton pressed a shoe into the grass next to his daughters' graves. He twisted the toe to leave an indention. "Here's where the grave will be. Are you listening, Gant? If you don't want to dig it, I'll get Neil Wease and Buck Murdock up here to do it."

"No one's digging that grave but me," Blackburn said.

"We're burying her in the morning, so you may need help."

"It'll be done and I'll do it alone."

"All right then," Mr. Hampton said. "I need directions to her father's farm, and the keys to Jacob's truck."

"I'm the one who should go."

"You've got a grave to dig."

"I'll do both," Blackburn answered. "Once I finish the grave I'll drive straight there. I'll drive all night if need be. For me not to do it would be wrong."

"No, Gant. That is my son's truck, not yours, and the only person taking it to Tennessee is me. I'm going to deal with these people once and for all and be shed of them forever."

Blackburn hesitated, then took the key from his bib pocket.

"Here," Mr. Hampton said, exchanging a pad and pencil for the key. "Make me a map."

"I got to sit down then," Blackburn said, but even on the cottage porch step, his hand quivered. He thought of the calendar at Jacob and Naomi's farmhouse, how it marked the expectation of arrival—just one more trick to make you think at least a few things could be made certain. When his hand stilled, he wrote the directions as best he could, gave the pad and pencil back. "I can't remember that last road's name, but it's dirt. There's a big white oak and you turn right. You'll follow that road till it ends."

"How long does it take?"

"Seven hours, maybe a bit more."

"Mrs. Hampton will come this evening to check on you. Like I said, if you're lagging, Wease or Murdock will help."

"I won't be lagging," Blackburn answered.

But as the truck disappeared down the drive, only the thought of Wease or Murdock digging the grave got Blackburn off the steps.

He went to the shed for the oilcloth tarps, then back for the shovel, mattock, and tamping rod, a plastic bucket that held the tape measure, string, and pegs. He made a last trip for the stepladder. Blackburn knelt beside the grave site, placed a peg, and freed the tape measure's tongue with a fingernail. He tugged the soft cloth like fish line off a reel. At exactly eight feet, Blackburn pegged the spot and strung the twine. He pegged and strung the other sides and cranked the tape back into its hold. There were newer tape measures, padlock-size, no leather cover, just polished steel with a button instead of a crank. Using them had never felt right to Blackburn, never more so than now. Unlike the metal tape, the taut cloth lay gently on the grass. Afterward, it didn't clatter back to its source. The old way was solemn, respectful. *A good grave.* That was all he could do for Naomi now.

And for Jacob too. Blackburn imagined him in an army hospital bed. He'd be happy, thinking how lucky he was to have survived and be headed home, believing that Blackburn had kept his promise to take care of Naomi. He picked up the mattock, tightened his grip on the grained handle, yet could not lift it.

Occasionally, Naomi had asked about his work at the cemetery. Blackburn answered but then changed the subject, afraid such talk might bring worrisome thoughts about Jacob. But one day while she studied, Naomi asked Blackburn to give her a word to look up, one she'd not know. *Obelisk,* he'd said, then spelled it and sketched one, explained its history. When she'd asked for more words, Blackburn said *tympanum, volute, spandrel, colonnette,* and Naomi checked the dictionary. It pleased them both when they knew a word that stumped even Mr. Webster.

One day he'd written *fylfot,* told her it could be seen as either a rising sun or a cross. When he drew it for her, Naomi said it looked more like a sun to her. As he was about to leave, she'd pointed to the sketch. *If something happens to me and this baby, will you promise to put one on my stone?* She'd said it in such a serious way, her eyes looking deep into his, that all Blackburn could do was nod. A normal sort of fear for a young woman soon to give birth. But now it seemed much more.

He thought again of Wease and Murdock and lifted the mattock. After a few swings broke the ground, he switched to the shovel. Dry dirt hit the tarp, made a sound like bursts of rain.

10

B Y ONE O'CLOCK the last of the lunch crowd of workers
had left. Having heard about both Jacob and the girl,
they seemed unsure of what to say so said nothing, which
was fine by Cora. She finished adding up tabs and set them
aside, looked out the window toward the cemetery. Cora had
already made the call to Sergeant Ross early this morning, been
assured that a hospital chaplain would convey news about the
death. Such quickness necessary, Cora had decided, because
it lessened the chances Jacob would contact the girl. Nevertheless, it was even crueler to have her son hear such words from
a stranger. *There will be a time when we make it up to him,* Cora
reminded herself, but that would not ease his suffering now.

A weariness came upon her, much deeper than a lack of
sleep. She still needed to check on Blackburn this afternoon,
call Greene about the name on the stone, and write the telegram to Jacob. There were so many lies to keep straight and
more would come. Like a long line of boxcars on a steep
grade, just one unhitched could cause disaster.

She remembered the morning Jacob was born. Weeks premature, his cries were like a mewling kitten. He was too weak even to suckle. An ambulance rushed him to the hospital in Winston-Salem. He'd spent a week in an incubator. Had it somehow started then, somehow ingrained in Jacob from the beginning that she and Daniel would always be there to save him? Besides the day Jacob stepped in front of the truck, at age seven he'd wandered into the woods behind the pasture. Daniel had led a dozen men on a three-hour search, finding Jacob not terrified at being lost but asleep in a laurel thicket. *This is no different, not really, just one more time we've rescued him from his own recklessness,* she told herself.

And not only himself rescued, Cora now thought, but anything he cared about. That too had begun early, his bringing home a baby robin fallen from its nest. She'd told Jacob to place it back where he'd found it, allowing him to think it might live though she knew his handling the fledgling ensured it would die. Wouldn't the truth have been better? Life is hard; some things can't be saved. Taking Blackburn Gant as a friend had come from the same impulse. And the girl, she was one more thing Jacob had wanted to rescue.

The store door opened and Sonya Davenport entered, feigning concern but there for gossip. *Let the busybody tell it,* Cora thought, fewer times that she or Daniel would have to. When Sonya left fifteen minutes later, Cora knew by nightfall much of the county would know the story. Specific details would expand and blur, perhaps help cover any slipups she or Daniel might make.

She checked the Borden Dairy wall clock, the black hands circling the cow's grinning face. Daniel would soon be at the

Clarke farm. She'd warned him that Naomi's father might be confrontational at first. Deference would be needed, not an easy thing for a man like Daniel. She'd learned that early in their courtship. They'd met at an ice cream social. Cora was the new math teacher at Blowing Rock High, come from Asheville, where she'd grown up, taught four years. At twenty-six, already viewed as a schoolmarm. Her seriousness and refusal to suffer fools limited her male admirers, but solitude was preferable to pretense. Cora's new principal introduced them. Daniel, already going gray at thirty, had a craggy attractiveness. He was courteous, but reserved, with no pretentious flourishes and, when he began to call on her, none of the silliness of flowers and chocolate. Instead, a man who talked to her of serious matters.

One of their first outings was to the sawmill, which he'd run alone since his father's death. Daniel explained the mechanical changes he'd made and Cora found them sound. She asked if he'd mind her looking at the bookkeeping. After studying the ledgers a few minutes, she'd made suggestions he'd taken. Their courtship was slow, deliberate. Eighteen months passed before their engagement. When Daniel's mother died, he inherited the sawmill. His sister, Sarah, inherited the store, which Sarah, already married and living in Charlotte, offered to sell. Together, she and Daniel checked the inventory, calculated the worth of the contents and the building, and then decided. All of it leading here, to this moment. Cora set envelope and paper on the counter, picked up the pencil. She carefully printed the words in uppercase, twice erasing sentences until she was satisfied.

DEAREST SON

WE KNOW YOU HAVE HEARD FROM THE
CHAPLAIN AND ARE MOURNING THE LOSS OF
NAOMI BUT ALSO KNOW THAT YOUR FATHER
AND I WILL DO ALL WE CAN TO HELP YOU
HEAL. THE CLARKES ARE VERY BITTER ABOUT
HER DEATH. THEY HAVE AGREED TO NAOMI
BEING BURIED WITH OUR FAMILY BUT ONLY
UNDER THE CONDITION THAT YOU NEVER
ATTEMPT TO CONTACT THEM. SO PLEASE
DO AS THEY ASK. WE ARE PROUD OF YOUR
HEROISM AND WILL DO ALL WE CAN TO HELP
YOU FORGE A NEW LIFE.

LOVE, MOTHER AND FATHER

Cora slipped the paper inside the envelope, wrote the name
and address, sealed it. Not wishing to push Parson further,
she called the sawmill, told Higgins she needed him to carry
a message to the telegraph office in Boone. She read it again.
Already the plan felt impossibly convoluted, so capable of
unraveling. Cora wanted the clarity of numbers, something
that, once solved, could never be altered.

11

THE AFTERNOON WAS COOL but Naomi had wrapped a quilt around her as she sat on the porch. Her father was in the woodshed, repairing a broken harness. *Aloneness.* So much of her life had been that way, and not just here. That first morning at the Green Park Inn, Mrs. Langston, the head maid, took her to the room she'd share with two other girls. *I'll let you settle in a bit, then explain your duties,* Mrs. Langston had said, shutting the door behind her. She came back half an hour later and walked Naomi and another new girl around the inn before showing them how to change the slips and sheets, dust and polish the furniture, clean the bathrooms. That evening Naomi had met her roommates. Deb was from Wilkes County, a farm girl too, and only months older than Naomi. Shy but nice. Connie was twenty-one and from Charlotte. She smoked and cussed and bragged about all the boys she knew.

Those first days at the Green Park, she'd learned a person could be lonely anywhere, not just on a farm. The inn was a swirl of voices and bodies, amid which Naomi in her maid's outfit was ignored. After their shifts ended at five, a lot of the girls, including her roommates, walked the mile into Blowing Rock. Naomi went too. It was better than being in a room by herself. The older girls spent their money on perfume and cigarettes, things Naomi wouldn't have bought even if she'd had the money, but they also went to the soda shop and picture show. She wanted to join them but couldn't, so instead passed the time looking in store windows. Naomi had never seen such beautiful clothes, more beautiful than anything in the Sears, Roebuck wish book.

Those town boys will try to lead you down a primrose path, Lila had warned. *You best stay clear of them, or you'll be carrying home more than just your maid pay.* Naomi had soon learned the truth of that. The boys and men at the pool hall leered through the tinted glass, sometimes stepping outside to beckon Naomi nearer. Others gathered near the soda shop, the cigarettes dangling from their lips removed just long enough to ask her name. *It's because you're the prettiest,* Deb said. After a month, Naomi allotted a dime each week to spend on herself. She'd study the picture show billboard before choosing either a sundae or the movie.

One Saturday in July, a young buck had come up beside her. He said she was too pretty to go to a picture show without a fellow, but he didn't say it in a smart-alecky way. When she didn't reply, he blushed. He told her he wasn't trying to get fresh, but if she wasn't waiting for someone it would be nice to sit with her. She'd looked at him more carefully then. Tan from working outdoors, muscles and calloused hands. But still cute, not rough-looking. A kind face, brown hair cowlicked, which made him seem boyish. As did the way he leaned his head to one side, as if too shy to look directly at her. Naomi surprised herself by answering yes. *My name is Jacob,* he said, and asked hers. But she didn't let him pay for her ticket or, once inside, buy her popcorn and a drink because she knew where that could lead. They sat in the dark and Jacob didn't once try to kiss her or hold her hand. Afterward, he offered to drive her to the inn. When Naomi said she'd not do that, Jacob asked to walk with her, and she'd let him. In the movie house she'd been nervous, sitting still, not talking, eyes fixed on the screen. But walking back they'd begun to talk, and it had been easy from the start. *July 28, 1949,* Naomi had written on a Green Park Inn postcard, *I met Jacib Hapton,* then placed it under her pillow.

Though *met* had seemed the wrong word, because somehow it was like they already knew each other so well. When Naomi mentioned what she felt the next morning to Connie and Deb, Connie laughed and said Naomi had seen too many sappy movies. Even Deb looked at her like she was silly. But the feeling of connectedness deepened as the weeks passed. By then she knew Jacob's family owned a store and sawmill. It hadn't changed the way she felt about Jacob, not really, but she found herself spending more time looking in the dress shop windows.

All summer she'd heard stories the other maids told about men who drank too much, couldn't hold a job, lied and hit them. Things Jacob would never do. Even the girls who had nice, handsome fellows said they wished their beaus' families had a lot of money. One day Naomi went into Blowing Rock's fanciest dress shop. The woman inside had looked at her maid's uniform and acted snooty, but that hadn't stopped

Naomi from taking her time, touching cloth so soft it seemed to flow over her fingers. The dress matched her eyes and looked to fit just right. When the woman came and asked if she was or was not buying the dress, Naomi had answered, *Not today*.

On the night before Naomi was to take the bus back to Tennessee, she and Jacob had parked at the Brown Mountain overlook. Boys liked to take girls there because people claimed you could see the lanterns of ghosts searching for a woman murdered long ago. A place to get a girl to snuggle close. But that night was more than kissing. Jacob said that he loved her and that they should marry. He'd pulled her tighter, his mouth next to her ear. *I swear I'll take good care of you, make you happy.* When she asked about his parents, Jacob said if they objected the two of them would elope. Naomi had promised her father she'd be back to help harvest the crops, but she thought of the months alone on the farm, and of all the pretty girls in Blowing Rock. For weeks other maids at the inn had been telling Naomi that a catch like Jacob would have lots of town girls waiting to steal him. Said in a knowing way, like Naomi would soon learn the truth of it.

So when Jacob proposed, she had answered yes. It was almost midnight when he'd taken Naomi back to the hotel, telling her he'd come to get her at noon. Deb and Connie were asleep but they woke up when she came in. Naomi shared the news and Deb hugged her.

"You got a good one," Deb said. "You'll never be making up a bed again except your own. Why, you'll likely have someone doing it for you."

"How soon after you said yes did he reach under your skirt?" Connie asked, winking at Deb.

"It wasn't like that," Naomi said.

Connie looked disappointed.

"Did he give you a ring?" Deb asked.

"No," Naomi said. "I think it just come of a sudden to him."

"And it can leave of a sudden too," Connie said. "I bet he hasn't told his snooty parents."

"He's going to tell them, but what they think don't matter. We'll elope if need be."

"When is all this supposed to happen?" Connie asked.

When Naomi answered noon, Connie asked if Naomi still had her bus ticket.

"Better hold on to it," Connie said when Naomi answered yes.

After Connie went back to sleep, Deb told Naomi to pay her no mind, that Connie would sour a lemon given a chance. But the next day when noon came and Jacob hadn't shown up, she figured Connie was right. Maybe his parents had talked him out of it, or he'd decided on his own. She'd picked up her grip and gone down the inn's marble steps. As she walked toward Blowing Rock, shifting the grip from one aching arm to the other, Naomi told herself she was nothing but a farm girl who knew nothing about men, or love, or much else.

She was about to enter the bus depot when Jacob's truck pulled in behind her. Naomi felt such happiness, even more than if he'd been at the inn from the start. *I had to get these first,* he told her, opening his hand. The gold rings shone in the midday light. As they'd driven to the justice of the peace that September day, Naomi kept rubbing her thumb across the bright gold. So much had happened so fast, she'd needed to feel its solidity. Now, eighteen months later, Naomi touched the wedding ring again.

The baby fluttered and Naomi set her hand on her stomach. *This baby will keep me plenty of company.* The sun felt good on her face, but now its light was sinking into the trees. Patterns of light and shadow laced the yard. She thought of the fylfot, and what she'd told Blackburn if something bad happened. *Don't settle your mind on that,* Naomi told herself. *You and this baby are fine.*

She heard a truck coming down the rutted road. At first, she thought it might be Lila, but through the trees she saw a glimpse of blue as the truck pulled up to the road's dead end. Blackburn had come back sooner than she'd thought, as if her loneliness had summoned him. She went inside to boil coffee. But when Naomi looked out the window, it wasn't Blackburn coming into the yard.

12

DANIEL STOPPED at a crossroads to double-check the map. He made another turn, soon came to a second crossroads, the white oak exactly where Gant had said. Almost there and not one wrong turn. *At least one thing easy,* he thought. As the dirt road slanted downward, the briefcase in the floorboard shifted. *It makes the transaction appear more lawyerly and official,* Cora had said. Yet she'd thought of the briefcase only as Daniel was about to drive off. His foreboding increased. So much had happened too fast for them to have thought out every pitfall. Even if they had, he still needed to convince Clarke and the girl he was telling the truth. Daniel always prided himself on being forthright. Now he'd lied to Mullins and Gant. Convincingly enough, it seemed. But he could not feign grief.

Daniel went over what he would do: show the telegram and say that he and Cora had also received one, then tell the father that they needed to talk but alone. The second part Daniel could not rush. He'd have to make the terms absolutely clear, which was why Cora thought a contract necessary. Not legally binding, but the Clarkes would be too ignorant to know.

Washouts and gullies rutted the road, which did not surprise Daniel. Nor did the absence of telephone poles. Several times the coffin shifted, a grating followed by a hard thump against the tailgate. *It has to be on the truck the entire trip,* Cora had said. In a mile the road came to a dead end. Daniel parked beside a decade-old Chevy pickup. Some dents but it looked to be in good running order. Before getting out, Daniel leaned his head back against the seat, closed his eyes.

When Daniel had entered the Western Union office eight hours ago, Parson was relieved to see the telegram in his hand. Then Daniel told Parson what else they needed him to do.

No, Parson said. *I can't be a party to that.*

Besides our gratitude, Ben, Cora and I want to recompense you, Daniel said, taking an envelope from his coat pocket. *It's five hundred dollars.*

That would just make it more wrong, Parson answered coldly. *Put that money away.*

Daniel had always liked Parson. Bringing the telegram to Cora and him was an act of kindness, but Daniel surmised it might also be an act of fealty. But as he placed the envelope back in his coat pocket, Daniel now knew better. Parson was a man of integrity.

After what's happened to him in Korea, Jacob deserves a second chance, Daniel said. *If what Cora and I are doing fails, you'll be implicated too, for what you've already done. . . .*

Parson's glare was his only response. Then he went into the back room. The teletype clattered. When he returned, Parson laid the reworded telegram and envelope on the counter. Daniel read and nodded. Parson folded and sealed it.

We thank you, Ben, Daniel had said, but Parson did not acknowledge the words.

After a phone call to Cora confirming the altered telegram, he'd driven back to Laurel Fork. At the cemetery Gant asked more questions than Daniel wanted to answer. The same at the sawmill. The coffin was ready but Higgins, a man who rarely questioned orders, asked twice if Daniel wouldn't prefer the girl's coffin be built with oak. Even then, Higgins didn't immediately set to work, as if still expecting Daniel to change his mind. Though both men did what was asked, they reacted in ways Daniel hadn't anticipated. Already, the specter that he and Cora had lost control of what would happen. And now he had to deal with Clarke.

Get it over with, Daniel told himself. He lifted the briefcase and got out, checked that the tarp concealed the coffin. Beside the creek, Daniel paused. The pasture's fence posts were upright, barbed wire taut. In the fields, long crop rows laid out straight as train track. A small yard, well kept. The biggest surprise was the house. Small, two bedrooms at most, but no loose drainpipes or peeling paint, no boarded-up windows. Ricks of firewood stacked tight on the porch. Even the small bridge showed care and pride—stone footings, sturdy oak beams and planks, not poplar or pine. Nothing slovenly.

A lanky gray-haired man, surely the father, came out of a shed with a feed pail and headed toward the barn. Clean-shaven, bib overalls patched but clean. Even the way he walked, not slouching but upright, confirmed Daniel and

Cora's misjudgment. Clarke was a proud man. The transaction would need to be handled firmly but with respect. Nevertheless, a new truck or tractor, more cattle, also made a poor man proud.

Smoke rose from the chimney, so the girl was likely inside. *If I just turn around, have Parson send the real telegram, maybe there is another way.* But by now word would have spread through town that Jacob Hampton's wife was dead. Too much done to be undone.

Clarke emerged from the barn, saw Daniel, and came toward him with no warmth in his face. But when he noticed the telegram in Daniel's free hand, Clarke's stride shortened and, still yards away, he stopped. It was Daniel who closed the distance between them.

"You know its meaning," Daniel said, handing the sealed telegram to Clarke, unsure if the man could read until he noticed the glasses in Clarke's bib pocket.

Clarke saw the sender, grimaced. The girl's face appeared in the front window, but she didn't come out as her father, his back to her, opened the telegram. Clarke read, then raised his eyes to meet Daniel's.

"The army sent you one too?"

Daniel nodded.

"And you done read yours?"

"Yes."

"I knowed it would never end good," Clarke said, gazing at the ground as he shook his head. "If she'd minded me . . ."

He looked down a few more moments before raising his eyes to meet Daniel's. The hostility and suspicion were replaced by a deeper sharing.

"I'm sorry about your so—"

"I'm not here for that," Daniel interrupted, nodding at the briefcase. "We've got matters that need to be made clear."

Clarke's head tilted sidewise, a look of curiosity that hardened into disdain. Any sympathy in his eyes expired. He placed the telegram in his pocket, glanced back at the house before turning his attention to Daniel.

"What's needing to be made clear?"

"About what happens now, a financial understanding," Daniel answered, "something with signatures."

"Signatures," Clarke said. "You town folks are big on that, ain't you?"

"It's to protect your family's interests as much as ours," Daniel said. "They made only a few payments on their farmhouse, so the bank owns ninety percent of it. Jacob had about fifteen hundred in savings and the army's death payout is even less. The ten thousand dollars my wife and I are offering more than doubles that amount."

The words were hollow, but Clarke seemed not to notice.

"There is a condition," Daniel said, nodding at the briefcase, "but I believe we'll agree on it. I think we already do."

"Tell it," Clarke said.

"That if you or your daughter, the child, or any member of your family ever come near Blowing Rock or try to contact us or anyone else in Watauga County, either by mail, telephone, telegram, or in person, we'll come after you, and the child."

"You think your money and your threats—"

"We'll do the same," Daniel interrupted. "Neither I nor my wife will ever set foot in this county again, and we'll never lay claim on the child."

"No claim on Naomi's child," Clarke said, observing Daniel closely. "It's in this 'contract' you want me to sign?"

"Read it yourself," Daniel said, nodding at a workbench.

They sat down. Daniel opened the briefcase, set the brick-size packet of bills between them, and handed Clarke the paper Cora had typed and then stamped with her notary seal.

"I'm damn well pleased to keep a state line between your family and mine," Clarke said after reading the agreement. "Give me that pen."

There was more to do before tomorrow's burial, but as Daniel drove back, his thoughts turned inward. Humiliation, embarrassment, guilt—he'd felt all of these emotions in his life. But this was something more. In that moment when Clarke's gaze softened in commiseration, Daniel had felt shame.

13

D R. EGAN HAD WATCHED the two of them since child-hood, Jacob the one friend the poor boy seemed to have ever had. *Why haven't you suggested they veil that child's face when he's in public?* Suzanne Vance, an alder-man's wife, had once asked Egan. Blackburn had been eleven years old when his parents, newly arrived to sharecrop a farm in Laurel Fork, brought him to the office. *His leg's getting bet-ter but his face stays the same. We tried a doctor over in Wilkes but he couldn't do nothing. We come to see if you might.*

Poliomyelitis causing flaccid paralysis of the left leg and face. The diagnosis was easy, but there was nothing to do, though some mountebanks might claim otherwise. It may get better with time, he'd told the parents. The leg had, only a slight hitch in Blackburn's stride, but the drooping eye remained, the right side of his mouth pulled upward as if snagged by a fishhook. He thought of the times Blackburn brought Naomi for a checkup. He'd walk her to the office's front door, even if the sidewalk wasn't icy, then wait in the truck. Dr. Egan had seen him out there, watching for her to emerge.

Ruthie had noticed too. On a particularly cold day, she'd gone out and asked if Blackburn wouldn't prefer to wait inside. He'd refused. At day's end, she stepped into Dr. Egan's office, the no-nonsense veneer he'd come to view as part of her starched white uniform absent as she sat in the chair opposite his desk, something she seldom did. *It's so sad. I just wish there was something we could do for him.*

Afflicted, that was the word country folks used to describe those damaged in mind or body. There were harsher words, sometimes used unthinkingly, other times not. Afflicted was gentler, even in pronunciation, and those who spoke it often believed such individuals were gifted in some singular way. It might be playing a guitar beautifully, like Arthel Watson in Deep Gap, or calming stubborn horses, or simply a beautiful smile. Egan remembered Blackburn standing guard in front of the soda shop door, not moving as Daniel Hampton railed at him. Few men in town would have stood up to Daniel like that. Steadfastness, was that Blackburn's great gift?

As the streetlights flickered on, Egan thought, as he had many times in the last hours, of what he might have missed that caused Naomi's miscarriage. There had been no vaginal bleeding, nothing of note when he'd examined her uterus and cervix. However, she was narrow-hipped, young, and over-burdened with worry about a husband at war.

Miscarriages happened, their possibility hidden from the best of doctors, but Egan was so troubled that he'd called the Hamptons' house in hopes of more information. Cora had answered his questions with a brusque *Her father didn't say.* When Egan asked which county the hospital was in, she'd lost all patience. *Why does any of this matter now?* Cora snapped before hanging up.

Because, Egan knew, if he'd encouraged Naomi to stay in Blowing Rock, she would have gotten to a hospital sooner. It might have made a difference; it might not have. He had made mistakes in his practice, several fatal. At Bowman Gray, one of his instructors told his second-year class that each of them was destined to be a murderer. *Accept it as you would a mathematical calculation,* he'd told them. *Unless you do harm out of indifference or malice, Te absolvo,* the instructor had proclaimed, raised arm waving an empty test tube at each row of students.

If only it were that easy.

14

BLACKBURN HAD NOT LOOKED UP to track the day's progress. Nor had he stopped for water. He wore no gloves and did not fetch them when his hands blistered, hoping pain might dim his mind. He was halfway finished when the gate clanked. Blackburn climbed out of the grave as Mrs. Hampton approached. He glanced at the sky, saw it was late afternoon.

"You've worked hard, Gant, but will it be finished by dark?"

"I have a lantern," Blackburn replied, wiping his brow with a forearm. "It'll get done, but I been thinking. If the burial's in the morning, will that give Naomi's folks time to get here?"

"They've already said their good-byes," Mrs. Hampton answered.

"You mean they ain't coming?"

"That's right."

Blackburn stared at her.

"Who says they ain't?"

"Her father," Mrs. Hampton said. "He told us last night."

"Not a one of them, even Naomi's sister?"

"Yes, Gant," she snapped. "That's what he said."

Mrs. Hampton took a five-dollar bill from her skirt pocket. "Payment for your doing this."

Blackburn looked at the bill, then at the woman who offered it the same way she would have as if he'd been digging up a stump or septic tank.

"You think I'd take that?" Blackburn asked.

"It would have been wrong not to offer," Mrs. Hampton said, looking away as she placed the bill back in her pocket.

"You all wanted this to happen. I heard it said out loud with my own ears."

Mrs. Hampton's face reddened.

"You know, Gant, I can . . ."

Whatever threat or vouchsafe did not come. Instead, she walked back down the hill. Blackburn returned to work. Soon he struck roots of a tree likely felled over a century ago. Dry and rotten, but Blackburn used the tamping bar, allowing no shard to blemish the smooth walls. That done, he paused to straighten his back, his head level with the two stones beside him. On them no first names or dates, as if time's measure negated such brief lives. Only one word, *Hampton*.

That first day he and Jacob met, they'd left the creek when Blackburn checked the sun, saw it would soon be milking time. Jacob said he'd walk partway with him. As they'd approached the cemetery, Jacob had stopped. *My sisters are in there. I'll show you.* Jacob unlatched the gate and led Blackburn to the twin tablets. He told Blackburn his sisters had died long ago. *It's like even though I never knew them, I still miss them,* Jacob said. They'd stood before the graves until

Blackburn said he needed to go or his daddy would punish him. They'd left the cemetery and passed the church, the land sloping toward the barbed-wire fence. As Blackburn slipped between the strands, a metal thorn raked his hand, drawing blood. He'd reached for his handkerchief, but Jacob motioned for him to wait. Jacob brushed the heel of his palm over a barb. A thin line of blood appeared and Jacob and Blackburn clasped hands. *We're blood brothers now,* Jacob had said.

Blackburn finished the grave by lantern light. Instead of warming water in the tin tub, he took soap and a washrag and went to the springhouse. He stripped off his clothes and bathed using the outflow pipe. Above him, a few stars speckled the sky but the moon roamed elsewhere. Soon warmer nights would be filled with the sounds of crickets and tree frogs, but now there was only silence. The body heat stoked by Blackburn's digging dissipated in the cold water. He made a few last swipes with his washrag and dried off. He took a half-empty quart of buttermilk from the springhouse and went inside.

After changing clothes, Blackburn crumbled corn bread into the buttermilk. He chewed and swallowed but did not taste. He went to the bathroom, took a sewing needle and drained the blisters, poured iodine on them. The orange palms burned as if pressed to a skillet. When the pain eased, Blackburn went to the back room, lay down. His closed eyes saw the shovel blade stab and pitch, stab and pitch, the hole ever deepening. So deep Blackburn could not believe he'd ever find a way out.

.   .   .

The next morning he removed the tarp from Naomi's grave. Less than two weeks ago, snow covered the ground, but on this day spring was not only on the calendar but announcing itself with warmer weather. Blackburn went to the shed and gathered the planks, ropes, and shovel, placed them beside the porch. He had no suit, so instead put on his best shirt and a pair of corduroy pants, polished a pair of dress shoes passed on by his father. Shoes Blackburn never had need of until now.

He thought of the times Naomi had asked about Jacob as a teenager. There wasn't much he could tell her. Jacob had often been with friends in Blowing Rock, especially after he got his driver's license, while Blackburn had been busy caretaking or helping his father farm. Several times Naomi brought up Veronica Weaver. In a casual sort of way, she'd mention how pretty Veronica was, or that she knew Jacob had taken Veronica to their senior prom. Blackburn would shrug. He should have said more, he thought now, told Naomi that Veronica Weaver wasn't near as pretty and nice as her and that Jacob would have taken Naomi to the prom if he'd known her then. Or said the most obvious thing of all—that once Jacob did know her, he'd chosen Naomi to be his wife, not Veronica.

At ten o'clock Mr. Hampton's Oldsmobile came up the drive, behind him Buck Murdock driving Jacob's pickup. They parked side by side. Neil Wease and Bo Randolph were in the pickup's cab. The men got out and Murdock unlatched the tailgate, the chains clanking taut. The coffin was slantwise. No pall, not even a sheet to cover it.

"You already got the ropes and planks?" Mr. Hampton asked.

Blackburn stared at the coffin, his anger rising. Pine, not oak. Unvarnished, the lid hammered shut with twelvepenny nails. Secured no better than railroad freight, hauled with as much care. Blackburn could imagine the coffin sliding around the truck bed, the jolt each time it hit the metal sides. After all the insults Naomi had endured in life . . .

Mr. Hampton was speaking but Blackburn ignored him.

"Gant," Mr. Hampton said, louder. "I asked you a question."

Blackburn turned.

"The funeral service," Blackburn asked, "when is it?"

"There's not going to be one here, so get your ropes and planks."

"But ain't Reverend Hunnicutt coming, at least for a prayer?"

"No," the older man replied.

"She deserves better than this," Blackburn said.

Mr. Hampton did not respond, but Murdock stepped around his employer.

"You ain't family, Gant," Murdock said, "so leave the deciding to them what are."

"I'm the only one here that cared about her," Blackburn said, glaring first at Murdock, then Mr. Hampton.

"Look here, Gant," Mr. Hampton said. "We can do this by ourselves, so help us or get out of the way."

As Wease and Randolph pulled the coffin off the truck bed, Blackburn filled his arms with the tools he'd placed by the porch. He trailed Naomi's coffin through the gate to where Murdock and Mr. Hampton waited. *This is what the world is,* Blackburn thought, and it was as if everything in his life had been slightly out of focus but now kiltered into a final clarity. Blackburn climbed into the grave and spaced the shorter planks on the bottom, then set the three longer ones so that they bridged the grave mouth. After placing the coffin on the top planks, the men paired off to grip the rope ends Blackburn handed up to them. He pulled himself out of the grave and removed all the boards. The coffin hovered above the grave as if hesitant to enter. The four men released increments of rope and the coffin slowly sank. When it settled, the ropes were pulled free and it was done.

"I'm taking Wease and Randolph back to the sawmill," Mr. Hampton said. "Murdock's going to stay and help you fill in the grave."

"I'm filling it in by myself," Blackburn said.

"Look at how blistered your hands are."

"I can do it."

"Nevertheless," Mr. Hampton said, "Murdock's going to stick around just in case."

Blackburn didn't move, his eyes steady on the older man's.

"Something you don't understand, Gant?"

"She's going to have a gravestone," Blackburn said.

"Greene's already making it. Cora called him earlier."

"Then I need to show you something," Blackburn said. He led Mr. Hampton to the front of the cemetery and pointed to an etching. "It's called a fylfot. Naomi told me she wanted one on her grave marker. Mr. Greene knows how to do it. It's got to be done. I promised her."

"This is a family matter," Mr. Hampton said.

Blackburn's mind turned to last September, the rattlesnake he'd found coiled on one of the cemetery's flat markers. After cleaving it with a hoe, he'd picked up the two halves to toss away. The pieces still twitched, but what Blackburn remembered now wasn't that, or the smooth scales, but the blood that had slicked his hand. How cold it was.

"I'll tell Jacob when he gets home it's what she wanted," Blackburn said. "I'll tell him you was against it."

Murdock took a step closer to Blackburn, but Mr. Hampton raised a hand.

"I'll handle this," the older man said, and turned to Blackburn. "A small one, but otherwise that stone stays exactly the way we told Greene to make it. You understand?"

"Yes."

When Murdock and Blackburn were alone, Murdock spoke.

"You ought to mind your mouth around Mr. Hampton, Gant. Be more respectful."

"I didn't see none from him today," Blackburn answered. "Her that's in this coffin deserves more than he ever will."

Murdock glared at Blackburn, seemed about to say or do more, then gave a shrug.

"If you're hep on filling that grave *respectfully,* go at it."

Blackburn did not change his clothes. He pulled back the tarp and picked up the shovel. As he lifted the first scoop of dirt and cast it onto the wood, the thump of the clods made him shudder. Each shovelful would deepen the darkness between Naomi and the world. Blackburn sank the blade into the grass, held on to the wooden handle as if a staff. He didn't think he could go on until he looked at Murdock waiting on the cottage steps.

As Blackburn worked, he thought of things he'd planned

to do before Naomi and the child came back. Besides the tire swing and garden, he'd found two dogwoods for the front yard. Young trees but big enough to show out a pretty bloom. They grew behind the springhouse, and he'd have used the same shovel he now held in his hands to dig them up. The sound of the dirt falling soon softened. He worked steadily, eyes only on his task.

When Blackburn finished filling the grave, Murdock checked it and left. Blackburn placed the tarps and shovel back in the shed, took a brass urn from a shelf and polished it with salt and vinegar. In the woods, only sarvisberry bloomed, its white petals long and thin like feathers. Not near so bright and beautiful as Naomi deserved, but Blackburn placed some in the urn and took the flowers to Naomi's grave. Wiping away tears, he set the urn down, pressed it deep enough to hold firmly, then went to the cottage. Blackburn wanted to lie down, even if no sleep came, but instead he took the coffee can off the top shelf, counted out fifty dollars, and walked down the drive. On the porch at Hampton's Store, the old men continued to talk among themselves, as if this day was no different than any other. Passing the sawmill, Blackburn saw the Oldsmobile parked in front of the office.

As he entered town, Magill's Pool Hall came into sight. Billy Runyon's green truck wasn't parked out front today, but Blackburn remembered it pulling into Jacob and Naomi's yard. Troy Williamson with him, but only Billy getting out, dressed in his sharp-toed boots and satin-back jacket, hair roached and oily. Billy had slouched against the hood as he raised a beer can to his mouth, took a long, slow drink. Blackburn had stayed inside, hoping Billy might get back in the truck and leave. But he hadn't, instead finished the beer and took another from the truck, swaggered closer to the steps.

Come for a visit, Billy shouted as Troy joined him.

Only then had Blackburn gone out on the porch.

Go scare them ghosts in the graveyard, Billy said. *Me and Troy can keep this gal company.*

Blackburn was about to pick up a stick of firewood when Naomi came out the door and raised Jacob's Winchester 54 toward Billy.

You best leave now, she'd said, thumbing off the safety.

I bet you ain't shot a gun in your life, gal, Billy sneered, stepping forward.

Naomi pulled the trigger. A chunk of earth exploded at Billy's feet, dirt spraying his trousers.

What the hell, Billy shouted, dropping the can as he stumbled backward and fell. Troy climbed back into the truck, crouching on the floorboard as Billy staggered to his feet.

Naomi ejected the shell, let it hit the porch with a soft clink, and rammed the bolt forward to load another round.

I'll geld you with the next one, she said, leveling the barrel at Billy's crotch.

I'm going, Billy pleaded, backpedaling toward the cab. He scrambled inside, slammed the door shut. The truck careened out of the yard and onto the road.

No, it shouldn't have come to that. He could have picked up a stick of firewood as soon as Billy drove up, not given him the chance to get out. But Blackburn hadn't, and he knew Naomi, like Billy, had believed he'd do nothing.

Blackburn followed Morris Street to a low wooden building, GREENE'S MONUMENTS on the shingle. The wide un-railed porch was cluttered with hewn stones of various shapes and sizes. Some stood alone while others piled against one another as if washed up by a storm. Pedestaled beside the shop's open door, a blank-eyed marble angel rose above the disarray.

Someone coughed inside. Blackburn knocked and soon Robert Greene appeared in the doorway, his hands and leather apron powdered white. He took out a handkerchief and wiped his palms and fingers.

"What can I do for you, Blackburn?"

"It's about the stone the Hamptons ordered, the one for Naomi."

"It'll be done tomorrow afternoon," Mr. Greene said. "I was going to bring it up Friday with Ezra Parton's."

"A fylfot needs to be on it," Blackburn said, taking out the money.

"The Hamptons didn't say anything about that."

"I talked to Mr. Hampton. He said it would be all right."

"You certain?" Mr. Greene asked.

"Yes sir."

"I'll have to check with them first, you understand," the mason said, "but I'm glad to add one on. I'll not charge you nor them though. Bare as that stone is, a fylfot will give it more character."

"Bare?"

"They don't want anything but *Hampton,* same as the other two. Mrs. Hampton insisted."

"Naomi's name and dates should be on there," Blackburn

said, offering all the bills he'd brought. "I'll pay for a whole new stone."

"Without the Hamptons' permission, I couldn't put it up," Greene said. "It's their grave plot."

The mason seemed about to say more, hesitated.

"What?" Blackburn asked.

"Maybe it's for the best, Jacob being so young and them not married very long, that and all the ill will it's caused between him and his folks. Besides, he'll likely marry again, and that stone . . . I'm just saying, everything considered, it could be for the best."

Blackburn turned and left without a word.

As he walked out of town, a memory, not of Naomi, but of Jacob.

Two feet of snow in a single day and night. The following midday, snow yet falling, Jacob came up the drive, a burlap sack on his shoulder. He stamped his boots, brushed off snow and entered. Brought you a few things, he said, and began taking out items— tins of coffee, soup, and deviled ham, a box of crackers, a bag of oats. Momma said if there's anything else you need to let us know. Daddy wanted me to check if you're short on firewood. Blackburn said no, offered money that Jacob refused but did accept a cup of coffee. They sat at the table, drank coffee and played cards all afternoon. That was a Monday. Jacob was out of school all week, and each late morning he came up the drive, bringing with him rook cards and a checkerboard. Schoolbooks too, because he'd promised his parents he'd study at least an hour, but Jacob never took them from the backpack.

He'd seen snow globes in store windows, and it was like for a week Blackburn had been inside one, every troublesome thing kept outside. Blackburn couldn't imagine such a care-free time ever coming again, for him or Jacob.

Once back at Laurel Fork, he entered the cemetery. With only the one small urn and its pale flowers, the grave looked forsaken. Yet it was Naomi's. Blackburn still stood graveside when Reverend Hunnicutt, dressed in his black suit, Bible in hand, came up the drive.

"I had a funeral in Linville and didn't hear about Naomi's burial until minutes ago," the minister told Blackburn. "I'm sorry for that, but I'm going to read scripture and say a prayer. I hope you will join me."

Reverend Hunnicutt opened the Bible, read from Psalms, then bowed his head and prayed. Blackburn listened, tried to let the words bring some comfort. Maybe later they would, but not now. Reverend Hunnicutt spoke his final amen and they were silent. Then the minister stepped closer, placed a hand on Blackburn's shoulder. The touch brought the memory of Naomi hugging him good-bye in Tennessee. Another memory too, Naomi linking her and Blackburn's arms as they'd walked down the darkened theater aisle.

"Jacob is going to be home in a few months," Reverend Hunnicutt said, "and he's going to need you to help him recover from all he's been through."

Blackburn nodded.

"We cherish the memories of those we have lost. Now we must also help the living," Reverend Hunnicutt continued, removing his hand from Blackburn's shoulder. "She is at peace."

After the minister left, Blackburn went inside. He undressed and lay down. Thoughts came but he was so exhausted his mind couldn't latch onto anything. Blackburn fell asleep, awoke hours later in the dark. He checked his watch. 3:00 a.m.

When Blackburn was fourteen, he and his father worked side by side hoeing, baling, feeding, mucking—the always something more a farm demanded. During a full day's work, they would exchange a handful of words. His father had never been much for talking, or smiling for that matter. If Blackburn spilled milk or missed weeds, his father's words were few but severe. When the job was well done, the most Blackburn hoped for was a nod, including on a blistering August Saturday after the two of them alone harvested half an acre of cabbage. Cutting the heads from the cobby stalks was work enough, but carrying the burlap sacks from the bottomland up to the shed was even harder.

On those summer Saturdays, his father left after supper to sit with other men who gathered at Hampton's Store. When he returned, he always brought Blackburn and his sister a bottle of soda pop. Blackburn never asked to go with him, never thought to ask. But on that August Saturday, supper eaten, he fetched his hat and a lantern and looked at Blackburn. *You coming or not?* he'd said, walking out the door without waiting for a response. His father had long legs and Blackburn trailed behind him. But as the store came into sight, his stride shortened until they walked together. Once there, his father stopped, took a nickel from his change purse, and held it out. *You ain't gonna get it for me?* Blackburn asked. His father shook his head.

On the porch, the men Blackburn passed barely acknowledged him, though all spoke or nodded to his father. Inside,

Mrs. Hampton was behind the counter. His father tipped his hat before turning to the metal drink box. Blackburn watched him lift the lid, peer at the metal caps before shoving his hand into the gray slush, fetching out a green bottle with 7UP on its side. After freeing the cap, his father took a swallow as if testing the drink's quality, then paid and went outside. Blackburn read the cap names. Some he'd never tasted—Cheerwine, Nehi, Yoohoo. Each time he pulled a bottle from the slush, the surrounding caps swayed like fishing bobbers. He settled on a Cheerwine, gave Mrs. Hampton the nickel, and went out. His father leaned against the porch rail. The chairs were filled, so several men perched beside his father on the railing. Others sat on the steps, leaving a gap for customers to pass. Blackburn went down the steps. Wooden drink crates were stacked beside the porch and Blackburn turned one on its side and sat. The men spoke of crops and weather, told a few jokes and tall tales. At eight o'clock Mrs. Hampton turned off the lights and locked the door, but the men lingered. The darkness made the men quieter, often attentive to a single voice. Later Blackburn would feel something similar when the Yonahlossee's houselights dimmed.

On the third Saturday night, a new man joined the regulars. As Blackburn passed, he'd elbowed the fellow beside him, spoke, and then laughed. His father told Blackburn to go on inside, but through the screen door he heard him clearly. *That's my son and he's already twice the man you'll ever be. If you say another word to or about him, I swear before God one or the both of us will end up in the hospital or a casket. You understand?* The stranger answered *Yes sir.* His father had come in the store then, got his 7UP but waited until Blackburn bought his drink. They went back out together. The chairs of the stranger and the man who sat beside him were empty. *Which one you want?* his father had asked.

Blackburn rose from the cot, took two quilts from the closet, and went to the cemetery. Wind stirred the tree branches and the weathervane creaked. A truck came up Laurel Fork Road, passed on. The wind stilled and the world grew silent. Blackburn wrapped the quilts around himself and lay down by Naomi's grave.

"You're not alone," he whispered.

15

T HE MORNING AFTER SURGERY, the morphine drip removed, unreeling images coalesced into memory: the fight, the hours under the bank, crossing the river, the oxcart ride to a MASH unit, days there then the helicopter and airplane flight. Jacob looked around the room, its whitewashed cleanliness startling after a month of grime. A hospital, not in Korea but Japan. A nurse came and took his temperature, checked the stitches.

"Very good, no infection. I've got something for you," she added, returning with a manila envelope, his name printed on the outside. "It's a few things that belong to you. I can take them out and set them on your table."

Jacob nodded and she withdrew his cigarette lighter, dog tags, strap watch, and the letter he'd carried in his front pocket.

"Should I leave them out or put them in your drawer?"

"Put up everything except the letter."

After the nurse left, he was drifting back to sleep when the army surgeon came to his bedside.

"Your baseball career is over if you're a lefty like Ted Williams," he said, smiling as he inspected Jacob's shoulder. "It will always be weak but we'll help you get some strength and flexibility back. But it is your boat ticket home. I'd say all in all you came out pretty lucky."

Yes, Jacob thought after the doctor left, he was. All he need do was look around him to see men missing an arm or leg, or worse. Luckiest of all to have Naomi, who'd known hardship but, unlike his parents, hadn't let it embitter her. Surely a part of why he'd fallen in love with her. Walking back to the Green Park that first night, she'd talked about getting more education, how sweet her sister's children were. Happy, hopeful things. In those first months of marriage when they'd struggled the most, Naomi still believed their lives would be happy, if not in Watauga County, then some other place. And once he returned to her, they would be happy. Jacob understood that in a way he never had before.

After supper, a colonel came by. Jacob's commanding officer had nominated him for a Bronze Star. The colonel shook his hand and commended his heroism. Yet Jacob knew the ice could just as easily have given way beneath him. After the colonel left, he fell asleep and dreamed of the dead man swaying in the current. What kept the body from being swept downstream was the hair, long black tendrils locked in the ice. Something fluttered brightly around the man's neck. Dog tags, Jacob's name stamped on them.

He was brought to the surface by an orderly, a jolt of pain in his shoulder.

"You ain't there, soldier," the orderly said, burly hands on Jacob's chest. "You ain't there."

Jacob saw the white ceiling, heard a nurse speaking to the soldier beside him. A radio played Hank Williams's "My Bucket's Got a Hole in It."

The orderly removed his hands.

"Sorry I had to pin you down, mac, but you were going to rip those stitches out the way you were thrashing."

"I'm giving you more morphine," the nurse said. "You need to sleep calm."

Soon he could feel the drug. Men got addicted to it, and Jacob could see how, the sense of floating, everything worrisome, not just the pain, far away. All would be well, the morphine said softly.

Though groggy, Jacob unfolded the letter's single page, flattened the paper with his palm.

Dearest my Husband,

Im here in our house and doin good but for you not here. Its been cold of late and snow but not much else for news. Blackburn has made shur that I have food enough and the pipes don't bust so you need not fret. The baby is good Doctor Egan says. I miss you day and night and pray you return realy soon and love you with all my heart. I study my books as much as I can so I can write better to you.

Love
Your Wife Naomi

Jacob set the letter aside, listened to the radio. After a while "Guitar Boogie" came on. Arthur Smith was a Carolina boy, and it was like the song was dedicated to Jacob. Although wordless, the music still called him home. Ten weeks or so and he'd be back in North Carolina.

He closed his eyes and imagined getting off the bus. The sun would be out, the creek gurgling, and the woods brimming green. Every step would remind him that his world, the true world, had not changed. When he could see his and Naomi's farmhouse, Jacob would stop and kneel by the creek, place his hand in the current, let it wash all memories of Korea down the stream, first into Middlefork, and then the New River, the Ohio, the Mississippi, finally the ocean, where they'd sink forever. Afterward, he'd go to the house where Naomi and the baby waited.

The following day Jacob walked outside for the first time. He wore slippers and pajamas, and though the day was mild, he draped a jacket over his shoulders. After the cold of Korea, it was as if he couldn't trust any weather completely. He sat beside a fountain. In its pool orange fish swirled like watery flames. He leaned back on the bench and let the sun fall full on his face. They'd taken him off the morphine drip and the day's clarity matched Jacob's mind. Even after his parents refused to help Naomi in December, deep inside himself Jacob had still hoped he and his parents might reconcile, but now, as on the frozen river, Naomi alone was what mattered. They would move away, find a new life for themselves. They should have done so sooner, as Naomi had wanted. Perhaps go to Tennessee to be nearer her sister and father. No, Jacob decided. They could always visit but they'd live in a place there was no cold and no mountains. Every reminder of Korea, even geography, forgotten, undreamed.

Jacob got up from the bench. As he turned to go back into the ward, a nurse pointed out Jacob to a chaplain. The man came down the sidewalk toward him, a somber look on his face.

"I'm sorry, son, but I have some difficult news from home."

{ III }

16

THE FIRST WEEK OF JUNE, the Hamptons had said, so for five days, Blackburn expected a vehicle to rumble up the drive, for Jacob's face, passenger or driver, to appear behind the windshield, yet had Blackburn not been sitting on the porch steps, the day's obligations to the dead now done, Jacob might have slipped into the cemetery unseen. He emerged from the evening's gloam, face gaunt and hollow-eyed, left arm dangling.

Jacob wore no uniform, but instead a white dress shirt that, unlike the wrinkled gabardine pants and dust-speckled shoes, looked new. An olive green backpack was strapped across his right shoulder. Blackburn stood but did not leave the steps. At the cemetery gate, Jacob leaned and set the backpack on the grass. He stared at the cemetery's center. In the receding light, the new stone's whiteness glowed.

Jacob opened the gate and went in, walked slowly toward the grave on which Blackburn had placed fresh flowers that afternoon. Jacob stared at the grave a few moments and then fell to his knees. Soft grave soil gave beneath his weight. Jacob placed his fingers on each of the seven carved letters as if reading braille. Blackburn lit his lantern and entered the cemetery to stand beside him. The first time he and Jacob had met, they'd come to this same plot, soon afterward clasped hands to become blood brothers. Blackburn couldn't shake the feeling that the dead sisters, Jacob's wounding, Naomi's death—all were connected by a single thread. Blackburn could think of nothing else to do other than have Jacob know he was here with him. Minutes passed. When full dark came, Blackburn set the lantern beside where Jacob knelt.

"I'm sorry," Blackburn said, about to add he'd be at the cottage, but Jacob spoke.

"When I was ready to die on that river," Jacob said, his voice breaking, "she was the one thing I couldn't let go of."

Blackburn reached out, awkwardly placed a hand on Jacob's shoulder, withdrew it.

"I'll fix us coffee and something to eat. Give you a few minutes alone, lest you need for me to stay."

Jacob shook his head. Blackburn went inside and placed the kettle on the stove. He heated up crowder peas and corn bread, opened a tin of applesauce. It was what folks did at such times, usually at homes but occasionally in the church, every counter or table crowded with plates and platters and pitchers. To fill mouths because words were so hard to come by, he'd always thought, but now Blackburn sensed it was more. The deepest grief couldn't be shared, so at least some simpler thing needed to be.

When the meal was ready, Blackburn went to the cemetery. Jacob still knelt by the grave. Lantern light pooled around him. Though not yet summer, a few fireflies glinted among the stones.

"Come on inside," Blackburn said softly, and offered a hand.

As he helped Jacob to his feet, Blackburn saw Jacob's hand-print at the grave's center. They wended their way through the cemetery and out the gate, but Jacob refused to go into the cottage.

"I saw the truck down there," he said, nodding toward his parents' house. "You got the key?"

"No," Blackburn answered. "Your daddy took it."

"I got to know something."

"Let's wait till morning," Blackburn said. "You're wore out."

"I can't rest until I understand," Jacob replied. "I'll walk to Egan's house if I have to."

"Maybe if you talked to Reverend Hunnicutt . . ."

"No," Jacob said, "just Egan."

"All right, I'll walk down to the manse, see if I can borrow the car," Blackburn said. "I fixed you a plate so go in and eat."

But Jacob was still by the gate when Blackburn returned with Reverend Hunnicutt's Studebaker.

They rode in silence. When they turned into the driveway, the porch light flickered on. Dr. Egan opened the front door, shirt untucked, slippers on his feet. As he came down the steps, Blackburn wondered if he too regretted Naomi's leaving Blowing Rock earlier than planned. Or did doctors, even kind ones like Dr. Egan, get to where such things no longer bothered them? Jacob rolled down his window but did not get out.

"Why, Jacob," Dr. Egan said, leaning close to the window, "I didn't know you were home."

"Tell me why they died," Jacob said.

Dr. Egan glanced at Blackburn.

"Tell me why they died," Jacob said again.

"Why don't we go inside, son," Dr. Egan said. "Blackburn, come around and help me get him in the house."

"No, just tell me why. Now, damn it. I'm not getting out."

The concern on Dr. Egan's face deepened, then eased into a seeming calmness.

"She died of a miscarriage, Jacob, and a miscarriage can occur for many reasons. There can be signs that something's not right, but most times it happens suddenly. Nobody's at fault."

"Hearing I'd been hurt bad could have done it, right?"

"I can't say that. No doctor could."

"What if my parents had taken her in," Jacob said, "or I had been here with her, would she have lived?"

"The later in a pregnancy a miscarriage occurs, the more dangerous for the mother. She surely would have died here too," Dr. Egan answered. "When's the last time you slept, son?"

"I don't know," Jacob said.

"I've got some pills inside that will help."

Dr. Egan stepped back into the house. When he came out, he went to Blackburn's window instead of Jacob's.

"One should be enough," he said, handing him the pill bottle. "He shouldn't be alone tonight. Take him to his parents' house. Tell them to call me in the morning."

"I'm not going to their house," Jacob said quietly.

"He can stay with me," Blackburn said. "I'll feed him and get him to bed."

On the drive back, Jacob laid his head against the window, though when Blackburn looked over, his eyes were open. As they passed Hampton's Store, Blackburn thought of late April, Naomi a month buried without anyone, not even Lila, having come to the cemetery.

Have you heard from the Clarkes? Blackburn had asked.

No, Mrs. Hampton answered, not looking up from the ledger book on the counter.

It's just that . . .

Just what?

It's just that I keep expecting her sister to visit the grave, even if her daddy don't. I thought you might have heard something.

If she hasn't come by now she never will, Mrs. Hampton snapped.

You can't know that, Blackburn said.

Yes, I can. They moved away the first week in April, all of them, Naomi's father and her sister and her family. He said they were going to Michigan to work in a car factory.

But whereabouts in Michigan? Didn't they give you an address?

No address, no phone number, Gant. Why can't you understand they didn't want us to know. Clarke said that the best thing about moving so far away was never laying eyes on Jacob again.

It don't make sense them leaving, Blackburn insisted. They owned that land for generations.

Blackburn had never understood why, despite her husband's hot temper, people were cowed more by Mrs. Hampton, but as she raised her eyes to meet his, Blackburn did. Once he and Jacob had *to peel skin off their fingers after daring each other to touch dry ice inside a delivery truck. Mrs. Hampton's glare was like that. So cold it seared into you. In Blackburn's life, others usually looked away first, but this time he did.*

This is not any of your business, Gant. Buy something or leave.

Blackburn pulled up to the cottage and cut the engine. Once inside, Jacob refused to eat.

"Come on then," Blackburn said and led him to the back room. He gave Jacob water and a pill. "You take this."

Jacob swallowed the pill, took off his shoes but nothing else. He did not pull back the bedsheets, simply lay down. Blackburn got two quilts from the closet. He stretched one over Jacob and used the other to make a pallet in the front room. But instead of lying down, Blackburn sat in the chair. After a while he checked on Jacob. He was asleep.

17

AFTER JACOB AND BLACKBURN LEFT, Dr. Egan thought of the first time he'd driven to Lenoir to call on Catherine. As they sat and talked in her parlor that Sunday, he'd noticed on the fireboard a small but conspicuous wedding picture of her and her late husband. That afternoon Catherine told Egan about a widowed friend who'd refused a marriage proposal. Her friend had always believed the intensity of love shared with her deceased husband was unique, and that she'd rather live alone than risk knowing otherwise. Egan knew Catherine was testing him. He'd told her that as a widower he understood such a point of view. *As do I*, she'd answered. To the delight of the mutual friend who'd introduced them, Egan and Catherine began seeing each other. The wedding picture remained on the fireboard.

He drove to Lenoir every other Sunday. They ate lunch at the same small Greek restaurant, followed by gin rummy and conversation. In the late afternoon, they'd leave her parlor for the bedroom, drape their clothes neatly on the divan. Predictable, even staid, but pleasing. *Love.* The word had never been spoken by either of them, as if its unsaying inoculated them.

Egan poured a dram of bourbon and sat down. The bereaved always wanted a reason, a specific term to pen in a family Bible. They might even request a dignified Latinate word for, as they often put it, w*hat had carried their loved one away.* One elderly woman's kin, dissatisfied with *old age,* asked for another term and Egan almost wrote *Charon* for her entry. But he was fresh out of medical school then, still callous from mornings beneath the gross room's harsh rafter of lights. In that stark theater the dead—naked, nameless, ungrieved—awaited his glinting scalpel. Unaccommodated man. Once he lifted a heart from a cadaver and held it in his palm. He'd turned away from his fellow students to address the cadaver: *Well, my fellow, it's no longer working but it is intact. You obviously did not die of a broken heart.*

A sin to have done that, and one piercingly recalled three years later when Helen contracted pneumonia and hovered between life and death. Callow mockery rebuked him. *What . . . no heartbreak now?* Even decades later, Dr. Egan vividly remembered those hours by Helen's bedside. With all his medical knowledge exhausted, he had prayed. He vowed that if Helen survived he'd never take her for granted again. Eventually the fever subsided and the lungs cleared. Soon enough there were times he did take Helen for granted, failed her in many ways. But over three decades, there were always moments when he remembered those two days—the fear, the prayers, the promises. As he'd told his adult children at Helen's funeral, he had been blessed.

Not so for Jacob Hampton. Dr. Egan hoped he'd at least

assuaged Jacob's fear of causing Naomi's death. *Miscarriage*. A resonant word, linked so often to the lack of justice. After learning of Naomi's death, Egan thought about contacting the hospital where Naomi had been brought, could still do so if Jacob kept asking for a more exact cause. Would a few minutes have made all the difference? Doubtful, but not impossible.

Dr. Egan thought of his children, his two grandchildren. Each December they drove down from Minnesota and Virginia to spend time with him. On Christmas Day they would take poinsettias to Helen's grave. He had not told his children about Catherine, though he didn't believe they'd mind. Catherine had a son in Chapel Hill she saw each month. Except for cursory comments, they seldom spoke of their children. That too, he supposed, was only right.

He was tired, but too much had been stirred up tonight for sleep. Egan went into the kitchen and poured a second dram of whiskey. Keats had come to mind earlier, so he took the slim volume *Collected Poems* from the bookshelf. He sipped the bourbon, welcomed its inner warmth. As the night softened, Egan read of a young couple whose love, unlike Jacob and Naomi's, had a happier outcome.

18

J ACOB FELT BOOT STEPS marching in place above him. He waited for the enemy soldiers to move on but they didn't. The undercut's roof trembled. Dirt and sand drizzled down. Across the river, his unit called out to him. Jacob screamed for them to shoot at the North Koreans so they would flee, but the unit couldn't hear him. Then someone was dragging him out of the undercut. . . .

"You're having a bad dream," Blackburn said, his hand firm on Jacob's good shoulder.

Jacob's eyes swept around the room. A calendar on a nail, a bureau, an upturned crate for a nightstand. No pictures, no mirror. Windowless, the only light entering from the front room.

"Where am I?"

"The cottage," Blackburn said. "You go back to sleep. I'll be in the front room."

"No, I need to get up."

"Then I'll go fix us some coffee."

After weeks at sea, then trains and buses, it felt strange

not to be moving. All he wished to forget had caught up with him now. Jacob put on his shoes and went to the front room. As Blackburn offered him a cup of coffee, Jacob noticed the newspaper article tacked above the hearth: *Local Serviceman Awarded Bronze Star.*

"Here," Blackburn urged, still holding out the cup. "I'll fix us some breakfast."

Jacob shook his head, lifted the backpack onto his good shoulder.

"I'm going to get my truck key."

"Dr. Egan wouldn't favor you driving."

"It's not him who decides that."

Jacob went to the cemetery, knelt beside the grave. With only a few grass sprigs, the swollen ground looked scalded. Jacob tried to speak, but the words clogged in his throat like mud. A vibration as from a tuning fork began to prickle his skin and the numbness he'd felt since March increased. He got up, unsteady for a few moments, then fetched his backpack and walked down to the road and crossed.

As he entered the yard, his mother came down the porch steps followed by his father. On their faces more than smiles, a joyousness. When, if ever, had his parents been like this? The night he and Veronica came dressed for the prom? His first day of college? No, not in those moments. The day they'd heard about Naomi's death. Yes, Jacob thought, likely then.

"If we'd have known the exact time you were coming," his father said, "we'd have met you at the bus station."

"But you're here, that's what matters," his mother told him, releasing her hug and stepping back when Jacob didn't respond. "Oh, your shoulder. It's still hurt, isn't it?"

"We're so glad, so glad, you're home safe, son," his father said, proffering a hand that rarely, if ever, had been refused by anyone in Watauga County. As if Jacob didn't see it, his father lifted the hand higher, flexed the wrist to reveal more of the palm. "Please, son," his father said. "Let's shake hands."

Jacob looked at their confident, self-satisfied smiles. They believed him ready at last to be their prodigal son.

"I'm only here for my truck."

His father's smile dimmed as he lowered the hand.

"That can wait, Jacob," his mother said. "You've got to be famished. I'll make you some breakfast right now."

"Your mother's right, son," his father said. "You've been through so much. Dr. Egan just called. I was about to come get you."

"Why," Jacob asked, "so you both can look at me and gloat?"

Uncertainty clouded his mother's face. She glanced at his father.

"No, Jacob," his mother pleaded. "Please, come inside."

"Please, son," his father said.

A car pulled up at the store. The driver went onto the porch and peered into the window, returned to his car and left.

"Come inside," his father said, a hand on Jacob's elbow. "I'll help you."

"It's time for all of us to forgive," his mother said. "It's time for us to heal, as a family."

For a moment the numbness receded. He looked as deep into their eyes as he could.

"My family is dead, and I know you're glad of that." Jacob paused. "You don't deserve a child, not even one."

Disapproval, disappointment, spite—these Jacob had seen in his life. But this was new. His father's chin sagged. His mother's hand touched her stomach as if to quell a sudden pain. *So you can feel hurt too,* Jacob thought. And then it didn't matter. Words, feelings, the house and store, the trees, even the mountains, leveled into meaninglessness.

"We've made mistakes as parents," his mother said softly, "but we love you and we'll do everything we can to help you now. So please come inside, Jacob. Even if you don't eat, you can rest or take a bath or just sit. I'll get you fresh clothes. You can go to your room and sleep if you need to."

Jacob let himself be led up the steps and into the house. After decades of fires, the front room smelled of smoke. On the mantel was the photograph of Veronica and Jacob on prom night but also ones of him as a baby and at his high school graduation. On the lamp table, though in a glass frame, was the same newspaper article Blackburn had pinned to his wall.

His father eased the backpack off Jacob's shoulder and set it by the hearth as his mother led him past the dining room and into the kitchen. His chair was where it always had been. The sugar bowl and salt and pepper shakers were on the same checkered mat. Jacob sat down and his father placed a cup of coffee before him. Not speaking, his parents watched as he raised the cup and sipped. His drinking the coffee seemed to reassure them. In a few minutes a plate came with all of his favorites—gravy and biscuits, scrambled eggs, bacon. His parents poured themselves coffee and joined him.

"I can fix you something else, waffles or pancakes," his mother said, but Jacob shook his head.

As they drank the coffee, the only sound was the ticking of the Franklin clock. Jacob turned toward the dining room's open door.

"What's wrong, son?" his father asked.

"That clock," Jacob said. "I don't want to hear it."

His parents' eyes met, and his mother gave a nod.

"Sure, son," his father said, and closed the door. "Your sergeant wrote us. He told how brave you were, all that you went through. We're very proud."

Jacob ate and let his cup be refilled. He'd need energy when he went to the farmhouse and did what he'd planned for two and a half months. Already he felt the caffeine's lift. One more cup would be enough. His father spoke, the words tentative as steps in a dark room.

"What we wrote to you, about giving you the store, your mother and I have it all arranged. Lawyer Bennett has drawn up the papers."

There had been times when Jacob knew Naomi felt resentful about his inheritance being taken away. She'd never said it outright, but on their honeymoon she'd told him about a sapphire blue dress in Watson's Dress Shop, a pair of slingback high heels in Lutz's Shoe Store. He'd told her the day they eloped what his parents threatened to do, but she hadn't really believed it. In truth, he hadn't either.

"You forget, Father. I'm disinherited."

"We were wrong to say that," his mother told him.

"Everything we have will be yours eventually," his father added, "but we want you to own the store now. We understand you'll need time before you take over running it, but it is yours when you feel ready."

He waited for his parents' faces to reveal a satisfaction that some temporary inconvenience had been righted. Instead, they seemed to be seeking his approval first. No, not approval, gratitude. *Thank you so much for the store. Now that I have it I can forget about my wife and child.*

"But you don't need to think about any of this now," his mother said. "We know you're going through a very difficult time."

"You *know*," Jacob said.

His mother's eyes met his.

"We understand loss, son," she said softly. "There are three stones up there with *Hampton* on them, not one."

In the room's smothering silence, the passage of time was unheard.

"I've got something to do," Jacob said, getting up.

"If there's somewhere you need to go," his father offered, rising also, "I'll take you. You're in no shape to drive, son."

"Just stay here and rest," his mother said. "Your bed's got fresh sheets on it. You can get some more sleep."

"Your mother's right," his father said. "As much as you've been through, you need to rest."

"Please, Jacob," his mother said, trailing him into the parlor.

Key rings hung on a nail beside the door. Jacob found his set and freed them, then walked out to the truck, his parents behind him, still pleading as he got in the cab and pulled out of the drive. As he passed the sawmill, smoke rose from the stationary engine. He remembered the summer afternoons he'd worked stacking boards. Given the hardest job by his father, his parents expecting the heat and toil to send him scurrying back to a college classroom. Jacob hadn't let himself be broken, even earned a promotion to crew foreman. Yet his parents couldn't admit they'd been wrong.

By the time Jacob parked at the farmhouse, his hands trembled so bad he clenched them in his lap, hunched over them. *Get this one thing done and you're free not to care about anything on this earth again.* He got out and stood in the yard. The porch and steps were swept, the grass fresh cut. What looked to be the makings of a garden were in the side yard, but nothing rose from the tilled soil. Jacob raised his eyes to take in the house he hadn't seen in six months. No screen torn, no window broken, no loose shingle. As if nothing had happened, not even time. On the porch by the door was a cord of neatly stacked firewood, beside it a bundle of kindling. That would make it easier.

The windows stared back at Jacob. Come closer, the windows invited, look long and hard. All those cold nights, wasn't this where you wanted to be? Better yet, come inside—look in each room, each closet, call out her name and hear silence answer. But Jacob wasn't entering the house, even to destroy it.

He walked around to the shed and found the kerosene can. Only a quarter full but enough. He went back and up the porch steps. Jacob set the kindling atop the firewood and sloshed the pyre with kerosene. He heard a truck coming up the road. It stopped and a man yelled at him, but Jacob didn't turn around. He poured what was left in the can around the porch and on the front door. The truck went on toward Blowing Rock.

Jacob flicked the silver lighter's wheel. When the flame steadied, he held it to a piece of soaked kindling. The wood caught a moment, then smoldered. Jacob thumbed a fresh flame, held it out. Six more times before the kindling caught. The first piece burned alone for a minute before finally spreading to a second. Jacob went down the steps. He stood in the yard, watching the flames wave and thicken. Finally, the cordwood caught. Fire spilled onto the porch floor and slats began to burn. Smoke gathered against the wall and front door. Jacob waited for the house to catch. He wanted to see the windowpanes turn orange and shatter, wood char into cinder.

A siren shrieked toward him. Even when it gave a last wail and the vehicle swerved into the yard, Jacob did not turn. A door slammed, then a trunk.

"What the hell, Jacob," Sheriff Triplett shouted as he ran past and up the steps, blanket in hand.

He beat at the flames until the wool itself caught fire. The sheriff threw the blanket onto the grass, came down and stomped it as a truck swerved into the yard, two men tearing off their shirts to swat at the flames until the porch steps they stood on began to burn. A fire truck wailed into the yard. The porch was a raft of fire now, the beams beneath tendriled orange, the porch wall and front door blackening. As one side of the porch buckled, a fireman shoved Jacob out of the way and aimed a hose's brass nozzle at the door and wall.

Jacob rushed forward, tried to jerk the hose free. One of the men from the truck grabbed Jacob, pinned him to the ground as a second fireman began dousing the steps and crumbling porch.

Smoke billowed as the last flames dimmed.

"Damn lucky it didn't get inside," one of the firemen said as the smoke began to clear.

"You better cuff him," the man holding Jacob down said.

But Jacob was no longer resisting. Everything inside him had also been extinguished. He had to be helped to his feet. Sheriff Triplett led him to the police car and placed him in the backseat. The sheriff watched Jacob a few moments, then backed out and drove toward town.

"Aren't you taking me to jail?" Jacob asked, his voice barely a whisper as they passed by the police station.

"No, son," Sheriff Triplett said. "I'm taking you home."

19

JULY 28, the day she and Jacob had met, was still seven weeks away, but as Naomi lay in in the dark, she was already making plans to order the marigolds that would be set on Jacob's grave. Of course her father and Lila would try to stop her if they knew, but she could get the flowers delivered without their knowing. All it would take was some money and an envelope. Naomi thought about Blackburn. For months she'd expected him to visit but he hadn't. Even with Jacob gone, she didn't think he'd go to Florida and work in the orange groves with his family. Did the Hamptons forbid him to come? Or did Blackburn, like them, blame her for Jacob's death? Naomi wasn't sure, but she was certain that he'd nevertheless place the flowers on Jacob's grave.

Annie Mae. Nothing worthwhile comes without a price, Granny Dowd, the midwife, had told Naomi that afternoon she writhed in the bed, Lila beside her, patting Naomi's brow with a damp cloth. Lila had placed an ax beneath the mattress to cut the pain, but neither it nor the damp cloth and Lila's soothing words dimmed the pain. Vivid pain, so much so that

Naomi saw it when she closed her eyes—bursts like orange flames—as she'd sweated and pushed. Between contractions Naomi had tried to think of happy things, but all that came was more pain—the memory of Mr. Hampton coming out of the woods with his briefcase and the telegram bringing word that Jacob was dead. Lila had squeezed her hand tighter as Granny Dowd said, One more hard push, girl, and that baby's gonna blossom out of you and into this world. And Annie Mae had come, wet and squalling and ever more pretty than the prettiest flower. And still so.

Naomi reached over and felt the infant beside her, Annie Mae's skin smooth and soft as a dogwood petal. Lila said Annie Mae should sleep in a crib, but Naomi wasn't ready to do that yet. She needed to reach out in the dark and touch the child, to feel the rise and fall of her breath and know a part of Jacob yet lived. Naomi pondered what to write about tomorrow. In the last months, she'd filled three Blue Horse tablets, memories for Annie Mae's hope chest. Though she'd taught herself cursive, Naomi printed each word. The way the vowels and consonants lined up separate made the letters look sturdier. She'd written about the evening she and Jacob met outside the movie house, about their sparking and elopement, their first Christmas together.

But as Naomi lay in the dark, she wanted to tell Annie Mae about an ordinary day. *Or what had seemed so,* because now she knew it hadn't been ordinary at all. Maybe that was the saddest thing about life, that you couldn't understand, not really, how good something was while living *inside* of it. How many such moments swept past, lost forever. But not all of them. Naomi lit a lamp, held it near Annie Mae's sleeping face. She was growing so quickly. Every day Naomi noticed a difference, another wisp of hair, the deepening brown of her eyes. *Don't let this moment disappear,* Naomi told herself. *Hold on to it.*

She went into the front room and opened the tablet to the first blank page.

In the weekdays before I carried you inside me, we would wake up at 6 in the mourning and eat our breakfast. Then your daddy would take me to the hospital to work in the laundry room while he built houses in Banner Elk. Then we

Naomi set down the pen, thought again of Mr. Hampton that day. She figured it was something bad when he came into the yard, but as Mr. Hampton talked to her daddy he looked serious but not angry or spiteful. Then the two of them were signing papers and she'd wondered if Mr. Hampton felt bad about what had happened in Blowing Rock. She'd thought that maybe, like Jacob had always believed, his parents had changed their will back so he was no longer disinherited. Despite all the wrong the Hamptons had done, as she watched her father and Mr. Hampton, her thoughts had turned to cute rompers and Buster Browns and all such else for Annie Mae, for herself a satin evening dress. She'd thought of how special nice she and Annie could look the day Jacob returned from Korea. But then Mr. Hampton left and her father came toward the porch, anger in his face, but also sadness. He'd stepped onto the porch and taken her hand in his. *Daughter, I have grievous news.*

Naomi closed the tablet. She heard a cardinal singing and looked out the window. Dawn. Annie Mae would be awake soon, wanting to be fed. Think of her, of other such good things, she told herself. Like how the corn was growing tall, the green shucks topped with silky blond tassels, and the cabbage rounding out nicely, and nearer the house tomatoes plump and blushing. Everything, including Annie Mae, healthy and growing. Be grateful for that. But Naomi couldn't clear her mind of Mr. Hampton snapping his briefcase shut, the click of the metal latches. Telegram delivered, contract signed. In the hours after learning of their son's death, the most important thing for the Hamptons had been ensuring Naomi and Annie Mae, Jacob's child, were forever out of their lives.

But it wouldn't be *forever*. When enough time passed, Annie Mae would be old enough to visit the grave and what the Hamptons threatened would no longer matter. By age twelve, Lila thought. When it happened, Naomi and Annie Mae would go to the cemetery and they'd do so in broad daylight. A dark thought came to Naomi. If the Hamptons heard and did show up, they'd find Naomi and Annie Mae standing next to Jacob's and his sisters' graves. To whatever vileness they spoke, Naomi would silently accept. Then she'd nod at the three stones, set a hand on Annie Mae's shoulder. *Your children are all dead, but my child is alive.* Naomi wouldn't say such an awful thing out loud, but she wouldn't need to.

But Naomi herself could not wait twelve years to visit Jacob's grave. Lila was already telling her she had to get on with her life, for her and Annie Mae's sake. But Naomi had to visit the grave first. She had to tell Jacob how much she loved him, how much she missed him. She had to tell him about

Annie Mae, and how Naomi could see so much of Jacob in their child's face. She had to do that first, to tell him good-bye before she could try to make a new life. If she went real late at night, the Hamptons wouldn't know. But the getting there, the keeping of what she was doing from Lila and, most of all, her father, how to do that? She would find a way though. She would.

20

After the fire, Jacob hadn't left his parents' house for twelve days. When Blackburn went to check on him, Mrs. Hampton said he didn't need visitors and shut the door. Dr. Egan was keeping him sedated, Reverend Hunnicutt told Blackburn, adding that Jacob might need to enter a VA hospital. Now the doctor believed Jacob was doing better and the hospital wouldn't be necessary.

Blackburn wasn't so sure. For a week, Jacob had come to the cemetery each evening. He still looked bad, hunched, red-eyed, and pale. Hair uncombed, face unshaven. Shucking weight too, Jacob's clothes not so much worn as hung on his bony frame. *Broken.* Sometimes he'd speak, other times only the slightest nod before unlatching the cemetery gate and entering. He wouldn't leave until full dark, a flashlight beam leading him back through the stones. Each night Blackburn offered coffee as Jacob left the cemetery. He'd take it and sit on the porch steps but said little. Blackburn hadn't done enough for Naomi. Now it seemed he couldn't help Jacob either.

Maintaining the grounds filled his days. A gas-powered mower was in the shed, but Blackburn never used it within the iron fence. Besides the loud engine, the cut grass spewed onto the stones. But the push mower's honed blades were whispery, respectful, as Blackburn moved around the cemetery. There was also weeding and pruning, cleaning the church and, as the afternoon waned, gathering fresh flowers for Naomi's grave. In the woods they'd marked spring's passage like a calendar—bloodroot and liverleaf, then mayapple and trillium, bugbane and blue violet. Now that it had turned summer, the best flowers grew at the Ledford homeplace. The couple who'd lived there were buried in the cemetery beneath a single slab of soapstone. Time had effaced the engravings, but their names and dates were in the files: Mabel Ledford 1845–1911, beneath that Jonah Ledford 1848–1912.

Blackburn followed the path down to the homeplace. As the land leveled, wildflowers appeared, but Blackburn went on to where the trees ended. Despite four decades, a sense of lives lived remained. An orchard lifted its limbs above briars and broomsedge. A plow, rusty blade sunk in the earth, wooden handles upright, seemed waiting to resume. The opposite hill had been part of the pasture. Even now, milking traces streaked the sparse grass brown. Decades to make them, and sure sign of a family farm. *When you own your own place,* Blackburn's father had said, *you know the land and the land knows you.*

In late summer, the orchard's branches buckled with fruit. Though Blackburn might eat an apple or a handful of cherries, it pleased him more to sit on the slope above the homeplace and watch what animals the orchard drew. Birds, groundhogs, deer and raccoons, an occasional bear. In front of the cabin were flowers that had long survived the hands that planted them, violets and hydrangeas and torch-bright tiger lilies. Later bee balm and black-eyed Susans would bloom, but no marigolds. Blackburn gathered enough lilies to place on the Ledfords' grave as well. He paused before the cabin. The tin roof had folded in on itself, but the corbeled chimney yet stood, as if a gravestone for the house itself. A bluebird lit on the remnants of the ash hopper, fluffed its wings, and flew toward the orchard.

One afternoon Blackburn had told Naomi how much he liked coming here. She'd asked if it didn't make him feel sad to see something people worked so hard to care for go to ruin. But Blackburn felt no sadness for the place. It was as alive as it had ever been, but he did feel sadness that the Ledfords could no longer sit on the porch and see the orchard branches turn red and gold. It would have been all the more color-ful then, pumpkins and squash another fall brightening. If things had worked out, he could have brought Naomi and the baby to harvest apples, maybe spread out a quilt for a picnic. At the farmhouse they could pulp the fruit into applesauce for the child.

Blackburn walked back up to the cemetery. He replaced the urn's day-old flowers, then went to the shed for a vase. He cleaned cobwebs off the fluted glass, placed the remain-ing lilies inside, and set them on the Ledfords' grave. After watering the plants, Blackburn went to the cottage, washed up, and ate supper. A jigsaw puzzle lay uncompleted on the table, but instead he went out and waited for Jacob, flashlight in hand, to arrive. Blackburn looked around. This time of day everything grew still, as if the world was holding its breath until the night fell.

As before, Jacob passed with barely a word. He entered the cemetery and knelt beside Naomi's gravestone. Minutes passed and evening sounds emerged. Crickets and spring peepers first, then the toads' longer trill, last the bullfrogs in the pasture creek. When Jacob came out of the cemetery, Blackburn again offered coffee. They sat on the steps, sipping from the cups, not speaking until Jacob broke the silence.

"You ever seen the Brown Mountain Lights?"

"No," Blackburn said. "Heard about them."

"I've seen them. I took Naomi up to the lookout and she saw them too. It's where I asked her to marry me. . . . To have done it there, a place of ghosts. It's like I was tempting fate."

"You ought not think that way," Blackburn said. "The time Naomi told me about that night, she said it was as joyful a moment as could be."

Jacob's voice shifted. Though Blackburn couldn't see him, he knew Jacob faced him now.

"When did she tell you that?"

"The last time I was in Tennessee."

"What else did she talk about?"

"The baby coming, some flowers she'd planted," Blackburn answered. "And you of course, what you'd said in your letters. I told her some stories about things you and me done growing up."

They were silent. The night was getting busier—moon and stars showing out, the call of a whip-poor-will amid those of the frogs and crickets.

"Daddy suggested selling the farmhouse, said he'd do the

dealing part for me. I'm going to let him. It's them who've been paying the mortgage anyway. Besides, there's no way I could live in that house now." Jacob paused. "I saw the plowed-up ground. Were you planting a garden for her?"

"Yes."

"Naomi didn't mention it in her letters."

"I wanted to surprise her."

"Surprise her?"

"Just figured she'd like having some dirt-fresh vegetables."

A breeze came up. The weathervane creaked, as did the gate Jacob had left unlatched. Blackburn looked west, saw the sky glow a moment, darken, then glow again. No rain had fallen in a week so he hoped the storm might turn this way. Below at the Hamptons' house, the front porch light switched on, off, and back on. As on summer evenings in Jacob's childhood, a signal for him to come inside. Jacob ignored it. Instead, he lit a cigarette, took a deep draw, let the smoke out with a long sigh.

"Reverend Hunnicutt talked to your momma the other day," Blackburn said. "She told him you was faring better and that Dr. Egan said the same."

"Enough to where she's at the store instead of checking on me every five minutes."

"You heard anything from the Clarkes?"

"No, and don't want to," Jacob replied. "That old man never liked me. He wanted a son-in-law who'd work that damn farm with him. He blames me for what happened, Lila likely does too. He told Momma they never wanted to hear from me."

"I do wish they'd left a mailing address," Blackburn said,

then more to himself, "It don't make no sense her daddy leaving."

"Why?" Jacob asked.

"It already April and near most of his crops planted."

"They didn't leave then," Jacob said. "It was the end of March. Momma told me when I was in Japan."

"She told me April," Blackburn said. "I guess he could have got someone to sharecrop it, but still."

"Why the hell does it matter?"

Take it as a good sign he can get a bit riled, not just numb to everything, Blackburn told himself, but Jacob was aiming this anger at Blackburn, the one person who'd taken care of Naomi, who was still taking care of her. It wasn't fair. He finished his coffee, was about to get up when Jacob spoke.

"Daddy and Momma put the store in my name. They're wanting me to work a few hours, build up to where I can run it myself. They tell me to spend time with my high school friends, go to the VFW lodge. . . . Oh, they've got plenty of plans for me. That's one thing that hasn't changed."

As Jacob took another draw of the cigarette, Blackburn set a palm on the step to get up, but Jacob spoke.

"The last few letters I got, Naomi told me she could touch her belly and feel the baby kicking," Jacob said. "I guess you knew about that too."

"No," Blackburn answered after a few moments.

Jacob flicked the cigarette butt into the weeds and stood. Without speaking again, he switched on the flashlight and walked down the drive. Blackburn watched as the beam swayed, vanished, then reappeared across the road in the Hamptons' front yard. Blackburn stayed on the porch. After a while the wind picked up, and clouds began to dim the moon and stars. Night sounds grew tentative.

My family's been on this land four generations and I'm damn well not going to be the one to end that, Mr. Clarke had told Blackburn the afternoon they cut firewood. It didn't seem right for that connection suddenly not to matter. Even if Jacob wouldn't go, maybe he could borrow the truck or Reverend Hunnicutt's car and visit the Clarkes' farm himself. If someone was sharecropping the place, they'd surely have a mailing address. Lila, like Shay Leary's brother, might be uncertain which cemetery Naomi was buried in. What if years from now, Lila or her children searched for her grave. The word *Hampton* without Naomi's first name wouldn't be enough.

Land. Blackburn's family hadn't had any. Sharecroppers, who owned only a cow and truck, never the fields they worked. While at the Ledfords' homeplace, Blackburn sometimes imagined the acreage being his. He'd look the land over and decide which crops would grow where. It'd be nice to bury something and then see it rise up.

That was how Naomi told him the rapture would be. She'd said so in January, spoke of souls like long-planted seeds rising from the dirt.

Lila claims we'll be in the dark and of a sudden lift up into the light. I likely think it's true, don't you?

Blackburn answered that he didn't know.

But you hope it?

If we look the same as we do alive, Blackburn said, *I'd rather stay in the dark.*

Maybe all we'll see in that light is the good in each other's hearts, Naomi answered.

Blackburn supposed such a thing possible. On Sundays, as he sat on the porch or listened in the foyer, he heard Reverend Hunnicutt say much the same. Sometimes Blackburn watched the fireflies and imagined they were sparks of souls hoping to enter that light. Maybe a harder life on earth would make you more grateful for what came after. Blackburn pondered Jacob's words about the Brown Mountain Lights. The story varied, but some people claimed it was only one searcher who roamed Brown Mountain, a single light, like Wilkie saw above Shay Leary's grave. Would that searcher also leave the darkness on resurrection day?

Sometime after midnight, rain began to fall. An oak branch raked the cottage's tin roof and Blackburn stirred. In the haze of half sleep, memory of a sore throat. That was how it had started that summer morning when he was ten. Nothing but hay fever, his parents thought, sending him out to milk the cow, then into the field to pull hornworms off the tobacco leaves. He was pouring sweat after walking a row. The throat worsened and his head began to pound. The field thickened into a glowing amber that his arms and legs slowly moved through. The worm can slipped from his hand. When Blackburn bent to pick it up, his legs gave way.

His father was in the adjoining field. He'd tried to call out but each word was like a claw raked over his throat, so he lay there, thinking of his classmate Sally Washburn, and of the word even the grown-ups feared to speak. One day two girls at recess laughed about how ugly the shoes and braces were, and Miss Jones overheard them. She'd told the class that Sally's braces weren't like regular ones made of steel or aluminum but actual silver. *Isn't that wonderful?* she'd asked the class, and they all agreed. *Sally the Silver Girl,* Miss Jones called her, but as they'd watched Sally hobble to a bench at recess, no student envied her.

As more time passed and no one came, Blackburn had grown weaker. His throat felt tighter. Unable to raise his head, all he could see was narrowed to inches. He became more frightened, thinking of children sealed inside metal tubes, and in coffins. One of his hands had been on the ground, and he'd dug his fingers into the fresh-tilled earth. *Hold on to it, and don't let go,* he'd told himself.

Blackburn's father found him an hour later, carried him to the house. His mother placed cold poultices on his head. The next morning the doctor in Wilkesboro confirmed it was polio.

For a week the world was a sweaty haze. Then the fever broke. But his legs no longer felt a part of him. Sloan's Liniment might help, the doctor suggested, so each morning and evening his father rubbed the ointment on them. He rubbed hard and it hurt at first, but then Blackburn would feel the warmth enter the muscles. His father didn't speak as he worked. At times, eyes fixed on the skin he kneaded, he seemed to do it angrily. His father rubbed some on Blackburn's face too, because his mouth had drawn up on one side. The eyelid drooped and Blackburn feared he would lose his sight, be like the man he'd once seen in Wilkesboro, tapping a white cane to find the world.

A month passed. It was Blackburn's father who made him try to walk. Even when he'd cried that he couldn't, his father made him leave the bed, holding him upright as Blackburn lifted one foot at a time. Gradually his legs strengthened, though the left leg lagged, but his face remained the same. All the doctor could tell his parents was wait and see and be grateful he can breathe without being locked inside a machine.

21

S JACOB RETURNED from an after-lunch walk, he saw a black Ford pickup in the driveway. It was Sunday so possibly someone brought to cheer him up, get him doing more than spending most of the day in bed. *You're healing,* Dr. Egan had assured Jacob and his parents on Wednesday, taking him off the phenobarbital. But all that did was trade numbness for grief. Closer, Jacob noticed a hay bale and pitchfork in the truck bed, a farmer, so likely here on a business matter.

Jacob walked around to the back porch, passed through the kitchen and on to his bedroom. He was about to close the door when his mother appeared.

"There's someone here who wants to meet you, son."

"I don't want to meet anyone," Jacob said, but his mother took his arm. "Well, you are anyway."

In the parlor, a man sat across from his parents, an empty cup in his hand. He wore a white dress shirt, thin black tie, and brown trousers, doubtless his church clothes. The man didn't seem particularly comfortable in them. His face was tanned, neck brick red. He didn't look that much older than Jacob, ten years maybe. On the coffee table was the letter Sergeant Abrams had written to Jacob's parents.

"You know who this is?" his father asked.

Now Jacob recognized him. His parents had pointed him out once in town, told Jacob of his heroism during World War II. The man stood and extended a hand that was missing two fingers.

"Seth Nolan. Good to meet you, Jacob."

They shook hands. Despite the missing fingers, Nolan's grip was firm.

"You've got no cause to be showing that letter," Jacob said to his father.

"It was written to your mother and me, son," his father said, turning to Nolan. "There's nothing wrong with parents being proud of their child. I know your parents are proud of you, Seth."

"Why don't you have a seat, Jacob," his mother said, making room on the couch. "Let me refill your cup, Seth."

"No ma'am," Nolan said, and turned to Jacob. "Your daddy says there's some quality speckled trout in that pasture stream. I didn't bring my fishing pole but I'd like to have a look."

Jacob hesitated, then nodded.

"There's a rod and reel in the shed," Jacob said as they stepped off the porch.

Nolan shook his head.

"I just wanted to get us out of the house."

"They been telling you about me, haven't they?" Jacob asked. "Not just that letter but how I've been since I got back."

"They didn't tell anything I'd not know from the look of you," Nolan answered. "You've been home a month now but you still ain't been sleeping good. Got no appetite, probably don't want to do nothing but lay in bed."

"It isn't just the war."

"I know about them up in the graveyard," Nolan said. "I can't help you much with that, but maybe some with the other."

They crossed the road, lifted strands of barbed wire for each other, and entered the pasture.

"No cattle?" Nolan asked.

"Daddy sold them a few years ago."

"You could raise a fine stand of corn on it," Nolan said. "Them cattle left some good fertilizer."

"Momma and Daddy always planned to build me a house here," Jacob said. Then, more bitterly, "They had plenty of plans like that. Still do."

As they crossed the pasture, the day's brightness fell full on them. They could see the creek now. Its surface glinted amid the rhododendron. They walked downstream. Here silver birch and hemlock lined the bank. Water slowed and deepened.

"Is that what you do, farm?" Jacob asked.

"Yep, corn and cabbage is the money crops, but we got most everything else—squash, taters, beans—you name it, for our bellies. Got a hog fattening up good for the winter. I swore that if I made it back from Europe, I'd never eat anything out of a can again."

"How long were you over there?" Jacob asked.

"Twenty-seven months and four days. After two years I

finally give up on the damn thing ever ending. Then suddenly I was laying on the ground and the medic bent over me and the chaplain too and all I felt was relief because I knowed one way or the other I was done with it and it with me."

"Were you married then?"

"No, I had a fiancée. But she got tired of waiting, hitched up with a fellow from over Goshen way."

"You're married now though," Jacob said, nodding at the ring.

"I am. Got three young chaps and another on the way."

They walked on to where a curve formed a pool.

"There's one," Nolan said.

Jacob saw the trout. Sensing their presence, its orange fins quickened. The trout flashed downstream and disappeared under a bank. They went to the next pool, peered into the water, saw nothing.

"Your coming for a visit," Jacob said, "it wasn't my idea."

"I know that," Nolan answered, "and I'll leave right now with nary another word if it's what you want. I ain't saying I know all of what you're going through, but there's some things I can pass on that helped me and might could help you."

"I'm listening," Jacob said.

"When I first got back, I hardly slept, woke up all sweaty and yelling if I did," Nolan said. "Every time a truck backfired or a door slammed, I'd be diving for cover. But it's mostly not like that anymore. Some men at the VFW claim they come home and that was that. Maybe it's true for a few, but for most it ain't near that easy. To my mind, war's not a thing you suddenly get *over* so much as you slowly work your way around. I farmed before I served and went back to farming soon as I returned. Being busy and tiredness helps keep your mind off darksome things. Going to the lodge can help, reminds you others been through it. In time, you'll figure out a few things that soothe you. When I'm plowing or walking my rows, I'll lean over every so often and grab a handful of dirt just to feel of it. Sometimes I'll close my eyes, hold that dirt to my nose and smell it. Tell myself, *I'm here. I'm home.* And then there's being married, having a family. Knowing you're doing it for somebody besides yourself helps steady you."

"I don't have that," Jacob said, "not anymore."

"I know you don't right now," Nolan said, his voice softening, "but that don't mean you can't have it one day. When that gal wrote and said she was marrying the other fellow, I thought I'd never get over it. I'm not making light of your loss. Losing a wife with child is so much worse. I'm just saying that what I got now, the best family a man could ask for, there was a time I'd not have believed it possible."

They walked on up the creek to the next pool. Nolan took a pack of Camels from his shirt pocket, offered one but Jacob shook his head. Nolan placed the cigarette between his right hand's two fingers and flicked his lighter, took a deep drag and slowly exhaled. Nolan peered into the water when he spoke.

"We can head back if you like."

Jacob hesitated, fearing if he started talking he'd be unable to stop. Nolan finished his cigarette, but he did not turn to leave.

"It isn't only what happened to Naomi and our baby."

"I'm listening," Nolan said.

The words felt so solid. He didn't know if he could get them out, that he might strangle on them.

"I killed a man over there. I think about him . . . about me killing him. I dream about him."

Nolan's eyes remained fixed on the creek.

"I've done that, the dreaming about them," Nolan replied, the words spoken slowly. "It still happens. Sometimes the dream is so real it's like I've killed them again. Here's the thing. Bad as it was, I tell myself whatever I done over there wasn't my choosing. I didn't start that damn war and I didn't ask to be in it. I only done what this country ordered me to do. I tell myself that. . . ."

He tossed his cigarette down, ground it with his heel.

"You a godly man?"

"I used to be," Jacob said, nodding at Nolan's shirt and tie. "Looks like you still are."

"Not in the way I was before I left," Nolan answered. "When I come back none of it made sense. Then one day my Uncle Zeke come to see me. He's a preacher over near Chimney Rock and was in the Great War. Got wounded in Belleau Wood. Anyway, I asked him why God allowed such to happen. I figured Uncle Zeke might give some sidelong answer like God works in 'mysterious ways,' but he come at it full bore, talked about how in the old time God got tired of the way folks was acting so he flooded everyone out excepting them in the ark. Then things got real sorry again so God figured to try something different and sent his own son down to see if folks might listen to him and straighten up. We know how that turned out. God says all right, then, don't pay me no mind. I'll sit back and let you do all the meanness you want and let you see where it gets you. So that's where we are and this time they won't be no ark nor son to save us in this mortal life. Anyhow, that's Uncle Zeke's thinking and it makes more sense than any other I've heard."

They went back to the house where Nolan wished Jacob's parents a good afternoon. Jacob walked him out to his truck.

"I appreciate your talking to me," Jacob said, shaking Nolan's hand.

"I was glad to, and I hope you'll come out to the VFW soon. I'm there most Tuesdays and Saturdays. Since next Wednesday is July Fourth, we're having a barbecue from five to seven. You ought to come and meet some of the fellers. Anyway, if you have need, I'm in the phone book."

Jacob went inside.

"You two have a good visit together?" his father asked.

"Yes," Jacob said.

"We're glad, son. We know there are things that happened over there, things someone like Seth can understand that we can't."

Jacob stayed in his room until supper. Afterward, he went up to the cemetery. People often spoke aloud to the departed, Blackburn once told him. But what Jacob had to say would be offered as it would be received—in silence. To the left of Naomi's grave was an empty space. Ever so easily, they could be lying here side by side. Had he known about Naomi and the baby that night on the river, he'd have given up. Blackburn would be taking care of them both.

Jacob thought about Seth losing his fiancée and how he'd likely known the woman longer than Jacob had Naomi. He thought about what the man had gone through in Europe. Seth hadn't lost a child though. Yet others had, Jacob knew, his eyes now on the two stones beside Naomi's. *Maybe your suffering isn't as special as you think,* he told himself. But Naomi had been special, and in ways his parents would never understand. She'd been through hard times too, losing a mother at four, growing up poor, only three years of grade school before her father made her quit, but unlike his parents Naomi hadn't thought the world was always out to harm you. His parents had been wrong about Naomi, but in the end they had been right about the world.

Back at the house, Jacob gathered Naomi's letters and read them in order, taking each out of its envelope, then placing it back before picking up the next. The last and most painful one had come to the hospital three weeks after the chaplain's somber words and his parents' telegram. Seeing the handwriting, he'd torn the letter open thinking what they'd claimed might be untrue, that maybe Naomi had suffered a miscarriage but only the child died, not her.

Dear Husband,

I hope these words I write find you safe and doing all else ways good. I am swolled big as a pumpkin but Lila says that is what should be at seven months.

Only then had Jacob reached beside the hospital bed to check the envelope's date and postmark, March 15, Pulaski, TN.

With that memory came another, more scalding. As he and Naomi were leaving Dr. Egan's' office, the pregnancy confirmed, Ruthie Burke came out with a pamphlet. *Now be sure to read this,* she'd said, holding it out to Naomi. *I'll take it,* Jacob told Ruthie. A woman in the waiting room snickered. They'd not spoken of it afterward, but a week later Naomi walked to the Blowing Rock Library on her lunch break and checked out two third-grade textbooks, trying to pick up where she'd had to stop school. Jacob helped her study. They'd ordered more books from a catalog, and by the time he left for boot camp she'd finished the fifth-grade level. Naomi was proud of herself, and he was proud of her too . . . but that moment in the waiting room.

Jacob placed the last letter in its envelope. He thought about the night they'd met, what it felt like to walk beside Naomi, how short the distance to the Green Park had seemed. They'd lingered on the hotel's patio. Jacob had wanted to kiss her but asked instead when he could see her again. When he returned home that night, his parents were in bed. Unable to fall asleep, he listened to the radio, every love song heard in a new, deeper way.

Jacob looked around his room. His parents had not changed anything—the pictures on the wall, the books on the shelf, the blue Blowing Rock High pennant tacked to the door. And the radio, its red dial exactly where it had been two years ago. As with the mantel photograph of Veronica and him, wasn't the unaltered room a denial of his life with Naomi, a certainty that the marriage wouldn't endure?

But the armchair beside his bed was a change, brought in the first night. When the dreams came, his father would wake him, then sit in the chair until Jacob went back to sleep. Jacob put Naomi's letters away, took a sleeping pill from the bottle on his desk, and went to the kitchen for a glass of water. One was supposed to be enough, but sometimes he took two, hoping it would offer sleep so black no dream could enter. Pills, the overhead and hall lights left on, yet still the dreams found a way in. Most always he was under the ice. Sometimes alone, sometimes with the North Korean soldier. He'd wake up gasping for air, drenched in sweat, his father's face above him. *You're safe, you're home,* his father would tell him. Jacob thought about what Seth Nolan had said about keeping busy. Just try it a day, a few hours, he told himself.

22

O N MONDAY MORNING Jacob dressed in his dungarees and a white camp-collar shirt, planning to go up to the store for at least an hour. But when his mother took the keys off their peg, he did not rise from the breakfast table to join her, even when she paused before leaving. She went on, not saying anything. Tuesday morning, however, he did get up and they walked to the store together. She didn't ask him to do anything, but when the store got busy, Jacob fetched items customers couldn't reach, filled gaps in the shelves and metal drink box. But midmorning the walls began narrowing around him. Customers kept asking how he was doing and wishing him well, including folks who'd frowned at him and Naomi a year ago. He left by the back entrance. The next day he stayed until noon.

As the week passed, his mother had Jacob take on more responsibilities. While growing up, he'd spent enough time around the store to have learned most of what he needed to know. When salesmen and deliverymen appeared, his mother told them it was Jacob's store now, had him do the payments and paperwork. On Saturday she left him alone much of the afternoon. Sweat soaked his shirt and his hands trembled each time he offered back change, but he got through it.

When Monday morning came, his mother handed him the store keys, told Jacob she'd help at lunchtime but otherwise to telephone if he needed her. You're ready, she said, and his father told him the same, so after a second cup of coffee he went to the store alone. His chest tightened as he unlocked the rear door and turned on the lights. Jacob looked at his trembling hands. *I've killed a man, nearly been killed. I've lost my wife and child. What's left to be afraid of, selling cigarettes and candy?* He opened the safe and took out ten ones, five fives, five tens and placed them in the register. He filled the coin slots, first half-dollars, then quarters, dimes, nickels, pennies. The Borden clock, which read 7:48, softly hummed. Jacob waited until exactly eight to unlock the front door.

Early morning passed slowly, a few deliverymen, a salesman hawking lather cream and hair oil. Farm wives came midmorning, some on foot. They carried wicker baskets or tote sacks. Like everyone else in Laurel Fork, they knew the store was now his. As Jacob tallied up their purchases, some said they were glad he was back from the war. Those who'd shunned him after the elopement kept their eyes down or offered overfriendly smiles and words. Jacob knew most of them had done so out of fear of his parents, but it was hard not to treat them with the same coldness they'd shown him and Naomi.

Agnes Dillard came by, and as she paid for her gas, she offered condolences for his loss of Naomi, the first person to mention her name. Unsurprising. On their first Valentine's

Day, Jacob had asked Mrs. Dillard for a dozen roses. Afterward, she'd refused Jacob's money, told him to think of it as
a late wedding present. Sometimes he and Naomi would go
into the flower shop together just to say hello. She owned her
own building, not renting from Jacob's parents, and didn't
kowtow to anyone.

The old men began to gather soon after. As if paying rent
for their place on the porch, each opened his leather change
purse, withdrew coins for a drink or tobacco before taking
his accustomed seat. The men watched Jacob curiously, seeing if, now alone, he'd treat their presence differently. Jacob's
hands still shook slightly as he made change, but he kept himself busy between customers, restacking shelves, sweeping,
patching a door screen. When he came out to stand among
the old men for a minute, they seemed to expect some pro-
nouncement from the new owner. But Jacob was silent.

"Going to be a hot one, son," Trent Waldrop said, nodding
at the Royal Crown thermometer by the door.

"Likely so," Jacob replied.

"From what I heard tell about Korea," Waldrop added, "a
man such as you might favor that to a cold spell."

"When I was in them trenches during the Great War,"
Norman West said, "you're talking some blue-ribbon misery.
We was bedaubed in mud and shit and all the while that cold
rain kept falling. I'm talking for days. Yes sir, let that thermometer run red to the top and bust for all I care. You'll hear
nary a complaint from me."

Jacob looked up the ridge to where the church spire rose
above the trees. The old men lapsed into an uncomfortable

silence until a delivery truck pulled in. On its side beneath the word *Sunbeam,* a smiling child held a piece of bread.

"That poor young'un's had that bread in her hands near ten years now," Joe Miller said, "and ain't got but that one bite yet."

The other men cackled as the deliveryman and Jacob went inside.

At noon his mother came to help as the sawmill workers began arriving. Jacob knew most of the men. They talked less than the women or porch sitters. Some merely nodded at the shelf behind Jacob and said a brand name—Beech Nut, Day's Work, Camel, Lucky Strike. Others bought tins of sardines or Vienna sausages, packs of soda crackers, candy bars and soft drinks. At one o'clock his mother left and did not return.

Midday passed. More delivery trucks and salesmen showed up, a few customers. Occasionally, Jacob looked out the window toward the cemetery. He thought about Naomi and then his thoughts drifted toward Blackburn, who sometimes acted like he was supposed to be the only one to look after Naomi. His doing so hadn't bothered Jacob at first. He was, after all, the cemetery's caretaker, but now it had begun to. Jacob wondered if some of the problem went back to Blackburn caring for Naomi those months he was in Korea. In a letter she'd mentioned Blackburn bringing her hot chocolate and how it tasted so much better than coffee. A small thing, but it still nagged at Jacob.

After five o'clock many of the workers returned, their bodies covered in sawdust and sweat. On a day like this, with the mill's stingy shade, sunlight baked them like a kiln. They lingered by the drink box, inhaled the frosty air as they might a pleasing scent. Several scooped a handful of slush to rub on their foreheads and necks. As a teenager, Jacob had always planned to work at the sawmill, loved to go there on Saturdays to watch the men as they sawed and stacked, operated machines his father made Jacob stay clear of. Jacob was good with tools and liked work that tired his body, not his mind like in a store. He envied them.

When the last man left, Jacob swept up the sawdust. He was about to empty the trash cans when Seth Nolan came in. He took a grape Nehi from the drink box, set the bottle and a nickel on the counter.

"Your daddy called and told me it was your first day running the store alone," Nolan said, nodded at the clock. "Looks like you've made it through just fine."

"I felt shaky this morning, but it got better."

"Mornings can be the toughest, but the clock hands keep on moving. Staying busy, it helps, don't it?"

"Seems so."

"Sorry you missed the barbecue, but some fellows at the lodge said you come by yesterday for a bit. They tell you we're having a band Friday night?"

"No."

"You ought to come, even bring along a gal if you have a mind to."

"My parents tell you to suggest that?" Jacob asked.

"Well, your father says you and Ben Weaver's daughter

was sweethearts for a while. I've seen her at their store. She's pretty as a fresh-picked peach."

Jacob glared at Nolan.

"My wife has been dead less than four months."

"I've not forgotten your loss," Nolan said. "I apologize if it sounded that way. Going to a dance with a gal don't mean you're trying to get a new wife or even a sweetheart. The main thing is the getting out, not feeling obliged to be miserable."

Jacob snatched the nickel and tossed it in the register. Nolan raised his hands, palms out.

"I'm not here to vex you," he said, picking up the soft drink as he lowered his hands, "but can I leave you something to ponder?"

"Go ahead," Jacob said after a few moments.

"Can't there be another kind of honoring someone you love? What would Naomi want for you now? Or you for her, if you'd been the one died?" Nolan raised his right hand with its missing fingers. "I don't want an answer. That's for you to ponder, and something else with it. We seen men, good men who were our friends, killed. We killed men. Don't we owe them, all of them, to make the most of life?"

At seven Jacob flipped the sign to CLOSED. He thought he'd made it through the day, but when he lifted the drink box to check what to restock, cold surged up and it all came back— moonlight, the river, the tapping of the knife blade. Jacob let the lid go and it slammed shut. As he turned, the world went slant. Gasping, he placed a hand on a shelf to keep from falling. The world slowly resettled. Breaths deepened.

The shelves beside him held candy and gum, as they had

in his childhood. Jacob touched each brand as he whispered its name: Jujubes, Mary Jane, Bit-O-Honey, Necco Wafers. Smarties, Kits, Saf-T-Pop, Life Savers, Charms.

Then the next shelf up.

Zagnut, Goo Goo Cluster, Valomilk, Snickers. Oh Henry!, 5th Avenue, Coconut Grove.

Then the top.

Bazooka, Dubble Bubble, Teaberry, Beech-Nut, Chiclets, Dentyne, Juicy Fruit.

He moved along the aisles, touching and naming, rebuilding the store, his world.

Last the cigarettes, the tobacco in them grown in North Carolina, some in this very county.

Lucky Strike, Viceroy, Camel, L & M, Old Gold, Pall Mall.

Jacob transferred the register's money to the floor safe. He swept the aisles and finished emptying the trash cans, mopped up a puddle of water beside the drink box. Before he cut off the last light, Jacob walked over to the gumball machine's glass globe. He looked at the colors inside, set his right hand firmly on the glass, and held it there. He remembered the world globe in elementary school, how the teacher would point out continents and countries but always let her finger return to the anvil shape of North Carolina. *And we are here,* she'd said, *right here.*

23

I N THE FOLLOWING WEEKS, Jacob visited the cemetery each evening except Tuesdays and Saturdays. His eyes held sorrow when he approached, but his hair was combed, clothes less rumpled. He had gained weight. They talked on the cottage steps, Jacob often asking questions about Naomi. How far along had she gotten in her math and reading, which days she'd felt good or bad, as if Jacob had to hear about every moment he'd missed. After claiming not to know about the baby kicking, Blackburn hadn't told Jacob another outright lie, but increasingly he'd leave out a detail or two in his recollections. Blackburn sometimes felt a bit ashamed of doing so, yet didn't he have the right to keep a few memories just for himself?

On this Sunday, Jacob wore khakis and a striped polo shirt, his face clean-shaven and hair fresh cut. He'd brought flowers, as he'd begun doing each Sunday, but these were a dozen red roses in a globed glass vase. July 28 was only a few days away so perhaps an early acknowledgment.

"You ought not trouble yourself buying that many flowers," Blackburn said. "There's already plenty up here."

"I wanted to," Jacob replied.

"Well," Blackburn said. "That vase looks to tip over easy. Hand it to me and I'll set it in the ground good."

"I can damn well manage that," Jacob said, bristling.

"Sure," Blackburn said, "just offering."

Jacob set the vase between Blackburn's urn and the headstone, then stood by the grave, head lowered. This time his eyes weren't closed. He seemed to be watching for something, but whatever it was didn't come.

"How's it going at the store?" Blackburn asked when Jacob joined him on the steps.

"I get through it," Jacob replied. "It seems folks can't buy a nickel's worth of gum without saying things will get easier for me. I hear it at the house enough, though at least there Momma and Dad are actually trying to help."

Blackburn lifted his gaze toward the far mountains, saw only darkness. A good rain had fallen two weeks ago but not a drop since. Blackburn knew farmers stood on porches or peered out windows. They'd wait minutes hoping to see a distant glow bloom and dim like a fanned coal. If outside, they'd wet a finger and gauge the wind's direction. As Blackburn's father had done, some would even step onto the dusty road, sniffing for the charged coppery smell that augured a downpour. But the midsummer hot spell had ended, this night's air too mild to stoke a thunderstorm.

"What you were telling me about Naomi, about how things were for her," Jacob said. "I was thinking about that. Did she ever talk about us deciding to have the baby?"

"She mentioned it."

"Why did she bring it up?" Jacob asked.

"I don't remember."

"Try to," Jacob said sharply.

Blackburn flinched. *This ain't the army and I don't take orders,* he wanted to answer.

"Just that things hadn't worked out the way she figured," Blackburn said, keeping his voice level, "you being with her the whole time, that is."

"And I hoped the same thing. The damn army changed that."

Jacob jerked the cigarettes from his shirt pocket, snapped the lighter impatiently. When the tobacco caught, a firefly drifted close, attracted by the glow, then drifted away. The cigarette seemed to calm him, words and body untensing.

"You still having a rough time at night?" Blackburn asked.

"I'm getting more sleep." Jacob sighed.

"That's good."

"When I have a bad dream, Daddy gets up and sits by my bed, sometimes the rest of the night. I'd have never thought him to do such a thing, but he has. Ever since I got back they've been so good to me. Momma fixes my favorite meals and brags on the job I'm doing at the store. I know they're trying to make up for what happened with Naomi. But in some ways you can bet they haven't changed. Momma wants to work Friday afternoons and Saturdays to give me more 'free' time. Funny, isn't it? They couldn't wait to get me in that store and now they want me out. . . . They told me last night that it's time to quit wearing this too," Jacob said, holding the ring next to the cigarette's glow, "because it keeps me thinking about the past. Like only this ring does that. When I'm in Blowing Rock, every place I go has a memory of Naomi and me being there together. You can take off a ring and put it in a drawer, but you can't make a whole town go away."

Down at the Hamptons' house, the porch light flickered on and off. Jacob ground out the cigarette butt with his shoe. Blackburn thought he might get up and leave. But he didn't. They listened to the night awhile. In the last few evenings katydids had begun thickening the night sounds.

"I took Veronica to a VFW dance last night," Jacob said. "We weren't there but a little while before I told her I wanted to leave. It had to vex her, especially after she'd bought a new dress just for the dance, but Veronica didn't say a cross word about it when I drove her home. Anyway, I called her this morning and apologized. She was sweet about it, telling me she knew how hard it was for me right now. Veronica said when Naomi and I eloped she'd blamed our parents, because they kept pushing us together. She figured I'd taken up with Naomi just to spite them. But later, when she saw us in town and how happy we were, she realized I'd married Naomi because I loved her."

Jacob paused. He seemed to want Blackburn to say something, but he was silent. Talking about Veronica with Naomi yards away in the cemetery felt disrespectful.

"There are things I can't get straight in my head," Jacob said. "Seth asked me what life I'd want for Naomi if I'd died in Korea and she'd been the one who lived. I know I'm supposed to say that I'd want Naomi to marry again, have a family and everything else we might have had. But to love a person enough that you'd want them to love someone else instead of you . . . that's hard."

Jacob seemed about to say more, then didn't.

"Maybe it ain't about having to make a choice which person you love," Blackburn said. "Maybe a heart's big enough to hold both."

"Where'd you hear that?" Jacob asked.

"Hear what?"

"About a heart being like that?"

"I didn't hear it nowhere," Blackburn answered.

Jacob made a closed-mouth sound.

"What?"

"Nothing," Jacob said. "Your saying something like that just kind of surprises me."

Moments passed before Blackburn replied.

"Then maybe you don't know me near so well as you think."

"Hey, look," Jacob said. "You know I didn't mean—"

"I'm going in," Blackburn said.

Later, Blackburn tried to read but his mind couldn't latch onto the words. He went back out and sat on the steps. Yesterday had been scorching hot but he felt the cool spell settling both around and inside him. Polio made his body sensitive to such changes. That would be with him forever, he expected, like his face. Blackburn remembered his parents taking him to Dr. Egan. He'd played with the toy tractor in the waiting room before going to a smaller room with his father and mother, the tractor still in his hand. Dr. Egan had spoken to his parents and then sat on a stool beside Blackburn, gently touching his face. *I'm sorry,* Dr. Egan said to his parents, then turned back to Blackburn. *Why don't you take that tractor home with you,* the doctor offered, and his parents had let him. He wondered if Lila had given the toy tractor to one of her children. Blackburn hoped so.

He thought about his parents and sister in Florida. His mother and father couldn't read or write, so his sister sent an occasional letter with news about them, but she had children now so the letters came less and less often. At Christmas, his parents sent Blackburn a box of oranges, received from him a third of his yearly salary. Two years since he'd gone to see them, enduring eleven hours on a train full of people who looked for seats on another row, or gawked and whispered. Blackburn thought about what Jacob had said, and how those words were so much worse than what anyone on that train might do or say.

And Jacob was his friend.

{ IV }

24

As BLACKBURN STARED out the cottage window, ground fog purled around the stones. Grave markers appeared unmoored, as if they might drift away, leaving each grave nameless and undated. He touched the glass, guessed the outside temperature near fifty. *Blackberry winter* was what his parents called such cool summer days. He was glad there was no funeral. Mourners needed some brightness amid the dark clothing and sadness. Flowers and wreaths helped, but it was the sun that offered the most comfort. From this hilltop, the whole valley could be seen, an unfurling patchwork of farms and woods giving way to mountains appearing endless as heaven itself was said to be. On a dreary day though, the Bible's hopeful words sounded damp and gray, defeated. Nothing seemed certain but the grave's dark door.

But such weather was fitting for the anniversary, Blackburn thought as he sipped his morning coffee. The cemetery grass needed cutting, but that would have to wait until the sun dried it, likely afternoon if not tomorrow. He needed to repaint the spire and touch up the belfry before the church's homecoming, so this morning would be a good time to go to town and get what he'd need. Blackburn poured a second cup of coffee, went onto the porch as the fog began to unscarf itself. Above, a pinkish glow emerged out of the gray, so maybe the grass could be mowed today. Blackburn looked down the hill, past the store and at the pasture.

The spring his family moved here from Foscoe, Blackburn's father sent him to catch trout for supper. He'd been fishing on the edge of the Hampton property when Jacob appeared. Blackburn thought he'd come to run him off. Instead, Jacob guided him to the pasture's best pools, and soon Blackburn's stringer was heavy with fish. He showed Blackburn a pretend fort made of fallen branches, said that together they could build it up even bigger. It was only when Blackburn was about to head home that Jacob acknowledged his face. *Does it hurt?* Blackburn said no. *I'm glad it doesn't,* Jacob had said.

You can't forget that, Blackburn told himself. *Jacob had plenty of people to be friends with but chose you, sealed it in blood that day we clasped palms. Remember what he's been through, body and soul.*

Still, what Jacob had said last Sunday on the porch steps rankled, even after Jacob came the next morning and apologized. But to have said it . . . More and more, Jacob seemed glad to give people like his parents credit for helping him, forgetting it was only Blackburn who'd stepped up last December.

Blackburn heard a vehicle. Agnes Dillard's panel truck rumbled up the drive. As he went out to meet her, the florist

opened the truck's back door and withdrew a vase of marigolds. Jacob's order, Blackburn thought.

"I'm going to need your help on where these go," she said,
taking an envelope from her skirt pocket, handing it to Blackburn. "This came in the mail a week ago with a five-dollar
bill."

Dillard Flower Shop
Blowing Rock
North Carolina

No return address. The envelope was unsealed and Blackburn took out the single piece of paper.

For marigolds. Give to Blackburn Gant to put on grave
July 28. He will know which one.

The note was unsigned.
"Do you understand it?"
Blackburn looked more closely and saw the postmark.

Pulaski, Tennessee

Confusion narrowed toward certainty. Lila would know
July 28th's significance, so the Clarkes must be back from
Michigan.

"They're for Naomi," Blackburn said, "from her family."

He unlatched the gate and they walked to the cemetery's
center. The florist settled the vase between the tiger lilies and

the drooping roses. She tousled the petals with her fingertips, closing gaps.

"There," she said, and rose. "It's the first time they've sent flowers, isn't it?"

Blackburn nodded. As Mrs. Dillard drove away, he began to feel a bit of his burden lift. Choosing this day with its meaning, wasn't Lila, perhaps the whole family, showing they wished to reconcile with Jacob if not his parents? Blackburn thought of Shay Leary, whose spirit needed a brother to visit the grave to have peace. Mightn't Lila's presence also bring some peace to Naomi, something Jacob and him both wanted? Blackburn left the cemetery and walked rapidly down the drive.

When he entered the store, Jacob was behind the counter restocking the cigarette shelf.

"Someone had Agnes Dillard bring marigolds for Naomi's grave," Blackburn said, catching his breath. "There ain't a sender name but it's got to be from Lila. She knows today's date and what it means, not just for Naomi, but for you."

"Today?" Jacob asked, turning to the wall calendar. He gazed a few moments and then his face reddened. "What did the note say?"

Blackburn told him.

"If it was them," Jacob said, "they trusted you to do it, but not me. That's spite."

"It ain't that," Blackburn said. "They just didn't want your folks to know. The postmark said Pulaski, Tennessee. The Clarkes have come back and they're wanting to make amends."

"Back to what?" Jacob asked. "Momma said they sold their farms."

"I thought Mr. Clarke might sharecrop or rent his, but he'd not sell. And Lila and her family owned their land too."

"You're saying my parents lied?"

"I don't know. Maybe they got confused or something." But even as Blackburn stammered out these words, he realized something else. The Clarkes might never have left. "I'm thinking we should drive over to Tennessee."

"Why would I do that if they are there?" Jacob said. "They don't want to see my face again and that's fine by me."

"I'm just of a mind Naomi . . ."

The screen door opened and Ginny Watson came bustling in. *The hell with it,* Blackburn thought, and brushed past Ginny.

"Wait, Blackburn," Jacob said, but Blackburn shoved the door open so hard the coiled hinge twanged, a loud slap as the door swung back.

In front of the store, Blackburn paused. *Go get the damn paint,* he told himself. He began walking. Soon the morning turned muggy, the sun full upon him. He wore a flannel shirt, so rolled up the sleeves. As he passed near the sawmill, he saw the red Oldsmobile parked by the office shed. *Why wouldn't they lie?* Blackburn thought. *They've done worse things.*

As he neared Middlefork, Blackburn saw to the left where, among broken slabs of stone, small blue flowers bloomed. If you came upon periwinkle in woods or a meadow, Wilkie said a graveyard likely had been there. It had always struck Blackburn how something fragile as a flower could honor the dead longer than stone. Longer than memory too, a lot longer.

By the time he entered Blowing Rock, Blackburn was dripping sweat, growing angrier with each step. *You got to calm down,* he told himself, *think this all out.* The park was almost deserted so he went there, drank from the fountain and sat in the shade of an elm. He looked across the street at the Yonahlossee. There was a one o'clock matinee, not too long to wait. He'd be in air-conditioning and out of the sun. *No,* Blackburn thought. What he had liked best before was the sense of something shared. Gathered together in the darkness, most everyone found the same things sad or scary or funny. But he didn't want to share anything with the people in this town.

Or even be near them, so he crossed the street to buy the paint and head back. Mr. Weaver offered a smile and hello. Blackburn ignored him, went to the aisle where the paint was. Veronica spoke to another customer and didn't see him, which was good. He found the right color, grimaced at how the gallon paint cans were always heavier than they looked. The walk back was mostly uphill, and the day would only get hotter.

"For the church," Blackburn said, setting the two cans on the counter.

"How are folks doing up your way, Blackburn?"

"Still dead," Blackburn answered.

Mr. Weaver frowned.

"You know I meant the Hamptons," the store owner said, but Blackburn was already going out the door.

Work gloves would keep the wire handles from digging into

his palms, but when Blackburn reached into his back pocket they weren't there. One more damn thing . . . He thought how good it would feel to slam the buckets through the hardware and soda shop windows. Even if he got cut and bled like a hog, it'd be worth it. Except he'd be in jail, unable to take care of what mattered more. Another drink of water, then rubbing some on his face and neck, would help before heading home. Blackburn crossed the road, but children were at the park's fountain, splashing water, filling orange water pistols.

Once you get back, you can go to the springhouse, Blackburn told himself. *It's cool and dark, a good place to think things out clear.* He shifted the cans more toward his fingers, saw the deep red lines where the wire handles had dug into his palms. *Get going,* he told himself again. *It's only gonna get hotter.*

A whistle came from farther down the sidewalk, then again, shriller. Blackburn turned. Billy Runyon stood in the pool hall's doorway. He whistled a third time and gave a sidewise jerk of his head, as if summoning a dog. Blackburn could cross to avoid passing in front of him. Billy probably expected him to, but suddenly the effort to do so felt too much. As he approached, Billy stepped onto the concrete, blocking his path.

"You and me need some things straight, so get yourself in here."

Blackburn shook his head, tried to go around but Billy blocked him. Troy Williamson came to the doorway, pool stick in his hand, then stepped back inside.

"You don't want to mess with me today," Blackburn told Billy.

"And I said we're going to get some things made clear."

"We got nothing to talk about," Blackburn replied, feeling the wires digging into his hands, trying again to step around.

Billy stopped him once more, placed a hand on Blackburn's shoulder.

"You don't have to speak a word," Billy said, half guiding, half pushing Blackburn toward the door. "All you got to do is listen."

He'd never been inside Magill's Pool Hall, knew little about the game except that it drew loafers like Billy and Troy who, as Blackburn's eyes adjusted, reappeared at the back table. Maybe because of the time of day, the only other person was an old man sitting behind the counter. Blackburn watched Troy slide the stick between finger and thumb. A soft click and the black ball rolled into a pocket. Billy stood beside Blackburn.

"Damn good shot, ain't he?" Billy said. "Near about as good as that girl. But now she's dead and Jacob got himself lamed, so ain't nobody protecting you anymore. You best remember that."

"I ain't in the mood for your mouth," Blackburn said, the words low, almost calm.

"Say what?" Billy asked, his forehead crinkling.

"You heard me."

Billy looked over at Troy, who stepped back from the table, set the stick's butt end on the floor. Beneath the glow of the green-shaded table lights, the bright balls lay very still.

"You take it outside, boys," the old man said.

"We're fine," Billy said. "Just needed to get a couple of things settled. Right, Blackburn?"

No, but maybe one thing, Blackburn thought. After months

of tangled feelings, how nice it was that something would be made certain. In the long room's dim light, he felt almost at peace.

"Hey," Billy said when Blackburn turned. He grabbed Blackburn's shoulder.

Blackburn dropped the paint cans and clutched Billy's front collar with both hands, pushed him backward until Billy's head and back slammed into the wall. He sank to the floor as Blackburn's right side erupted with a lightning strike of pain, but before Troy swung again, Blackburn grabbed the stick with one hand and Troy's throat with the other. Troy let go of the stick, used both hands to free Blackburn's choke-hold, staggered back, and grabbed a billiard ball. Before he could throw it, Blackburn swung two-handed. A shatter of wood and bone and Troy fell. Clutching his side and moaning, he crawled under the table.

Billy remained on the floor, body slumped and legs sprawled like a child's poppit doll.

"That's enough, or I call the sheriff," the man behind the counter said.

Blackburn still held the jagged stick end as he stood over Billy. It would be so easy to pierce Billy's cheek, rip open the skin from ear to mouth. *He deserves it more than I do,* Blackburn thought as he knelt on one knee, told Billy to look at him.

Billy was still dazed but managed to lift his head enough to meet Blackburn's eyes.

"Don't you trifle with me no more, understand?" Blackburn said, nodding at the stick end, "because if you do I'll make your face uglier than mine."

"Okay, Blackburn, sure," Billy said, his head lolling to one side. "I swear it so."

"I seen who started all this," the man behind the counter said to Blackburn. "But if you don't stop now I'll law the sheriff on you."

Troy remained huddled under the table as Blackburn picked up the other stick piece, set both on the counter.

"How much I owe for breaking it?"

"No charge," the man said. "Him that owes me is under the table. He's the one lent it to you."

25

NAOMI REMEMBERED being held as her mother fed a flock of chickens. The birds flapped and clucked around them and at first she'd been afraid, but her mother tossed the corn wider and the chickens scattered. That and a few more smudgy memories Naomi wasn't even sure were real or something told to her later. *I wish I'd known Mama long as you did,* she'd told Lila once. *But can't you see I've got so much more to miss?* her sister answered.

Naomi had pondered Lila's answer often. She understood it in a way, but memories could bring you happiness as well as sorrows. She thought again of the day Jacob picked her up at the bus station. Before they got in the truck, he told her that his parents had vowed to disinherit him if they eloped. She'd thought that Jacob might be testing her, making sure she wanted him, not the Hamptons' money. *I don't care about that,* Naomi answered, and she hadn't, not really, but what he'd said was true. Mr. Hampton also fired Jacob from the sawmill, and they'd spent a week in a motor lodge before finding the house on Leon Coffey Road.

The first month had been so hard. It wasn't Jacob's fault, but it hadn't felt quite fair. That last night at the Green Park, Deb told Naomi she'd be able to buy the most expensive dress in Blowing Rock, one even most tourists couldn't afford. Spiffy shoes and pocketbooks, perfume and jewelry, and not caring a whit what it cost. *You'll be like Cinderella,* Deb had said. Later that night as she'd lain in bed, Naomi had imagined it would be like that. She and Jacob would come into the Green Park, him in a nice suit and her wearing the blue silk dress that cost more than a summer's pay of maid work. They'd order anything they wanted on the menu and afterward dance in the ballroom. The other guests wouldn't imagine that only a year ago Naomi had been scrubbing their toilets. The girls she'd worked with would know, though, and most of them would be proud and happy for her.

Instead, she and Jacob moved into a run-down farmhouse. When Naomi walked through town, hardly anyone was friendly. Jacob kept believing his parents would change their minds, and Naomi too for a while, but his parents hadn't. She did at least get a year-round job in the hospital's laundry, and Jacob got hired to help build houses, so they had rent money and food. Naomi hadn't minded the work. What bothered her was what Connie and some of the other maids would think. She imagined them talking about how Naomi thought she'd caught her a rich boy to marry but got tricked in the end, worried that some of the women she worked with in the hospital basement gossiped about the same thing.

Childishness. The same when she made Blackburn take her to town that day. Putting on lipstick and powder, wearing a dress, not the maternity smock, so people had to notice her belly. She'd lied to Blackburn about dressing up that way to look pretty. Or tried to lie, because Blackburn knew what might happen, had tried to stop it and likely would have if Naomi hadn't lied again by saying Jacob would want her to go. Put Blackburn in the midst of it. Worse, remembering the fall, she'd endangered Annie Mae. Yes, childishness, nothing more. But she wasn't a child now. She'd learned that the hard way, losing a husband, raising a baby alone.

Naomi wondered if Blackburn had placed the marigolds on Jacob's grave. Surely he would. Maybe sending the flowers would prompt him to finally visit, yet as she thought this Naomi realized another reason he hadn't come. The Hamptons would take Jacob's truck from him, spiting Blackburn for helping her. Naomi remembered the first time she'd seen Blackburn. Jacob had warned her beforehand about his face, so she hadn't looked away or caught her breath. But she understood why some people did. He was a big man, which might make him even scarier to some folks. Nevertheless, soon enough Naomi didn't notice the face, or how his left leg dragged a bit, as much as Blackburn's kindness. When she'd asked him to feel her stomach that day, he'd done it. A strong hand placed ever so gently.

Naomi looked out at the field where her father plowed. Everything was growing well, including Annie Mae. But what looked promising could always change. . . .

Jacob thought the chance to buy the farmhouse a godsend, the best sort of luck. It had been unexpected, just a moment when Mr. Matney mentioned a price so low that a mortgage payment was little more than rent. But fixing up an old house cost money. *Our house, no one else's,* Jacob had told her. She'd tried to look at it that way, just another step in what married people did. Naomi's worries went beyond the money though. Rawlings Construction was a big company, and Jacob's boss was already hinting about future transfers and promotions. Charlotte, Atlanta, even Knoxville. Married only six months and still getting used to each other's ways, Naomi feared day jobs and then working on the house would overwhelm them. They'd be tired and snippy, always worrying about having enough money.

However, the work only brought them closer. Together they made decisions about room colors and what went where. Even on their tiredest evenings, they'd look around and see new glass in a window, a freshly painted room. Blackburn helped a lot too. He wasn't like a real visitor, but it was gladdening to have someone else see all they'd done. Yet her worries about buying the farmhouse had lingered, especially when Jacob's boss offered him a transfer to Atlanta with a raise and promotion. But to start anew after just fixing up one house. Jacob still thought his parents might accept them, and Naomi still hoped he was right. So they'd stayed. She wasn't sure how army conscription was done, but since Georgia was a different state, if they'd left might he not have been conscripted at all?

An old house, built before the turn of the century. Broken windows, shingles missing, creaking floorboards. A place best suited for ghosts, yet she and Jacob had tried so hard to make it a place for the living. Naomi imagined the house slowly returning to how she'd first seen it. Abandoned for good this time. And before long a place that people rightly stayed clear of. Haunted, now if not before.

She wondered what Jacob's gravestone looked like. A single word on the daughters' markers made clear his parents didn't care about things like that. Blackburn cared, so he might have done more, though the Hamptons were hateful enough to stop him from doing so. *Five more weeks.* Then Naomi would go to Jacob's grave and find out for herself. She hadn't told Lila yet, but Naomi would have to in the coming days, all the while keeping her father from finding out.

There was so much to decide. She'd soon be ready to try for a GED. Once she had the certificate, Naomi wondered if maybe she could leave Annie Mae with Lila a few months and go to business school in Knoxville, learn typing and stenography and get a job in Pulaski. But if that didn't work out, the school and place to stay too expensive? Her father had been supportive of her book learning. He'd had eight years of schooling before he had to quit and always said if their mother had lived Lila and Naomi would have had at least as much. Sometimes he'd pick up her books, read them on the porch after supper.

But her father would be dead set against her going off to Knoxville, and Lila would feel the same way. She knew their arguments already, and what might not be spoken but nevertheless made clear—her father had taken Naomi in when she had nowhere else to go. He'd done so despite Naomi breaking her promise to return from the Green Park at harvest time, give over her earnings to help pay farm bills. He was owed, and in his and Lila's minds that meant Naomi marrying to keep the farm going. And yet, wasn't a child's father owed too? Jacob would want Annie Mae to have opportunities beyond the farm. Education, even college. As did Naomi, he'd want her to see those opportunities early in life.

But before anything else, she had to go to Jacob's grave. *A duty to the dead,* Blackburn said about his job. This was Naomi's duty, one that must be fulfilled before her life went on. She had so much to say to Jacob, about how hard it was without him and how much she loved him. Most of all, she wanted to tell Jacob about Annie Mae. Naomi could ask what she should do, and maybe somehow Jacob could help guide her. Once she'd asked Blackburn if he thought the cemetery was haunted and he'd answered that he didn't know. Now she wanted it to be.

She looked out at the cornfield, the stalks so tall that her father seemed to wade in green water as he moved up and down the rows. There'd been such a change in him. Her father had grumbled a lot about Naomi being back home, but then Annie Mae was born. Smitten from the start, he'd built her the prettiest cherry hope chest. Even more surprising was how he loved to rock Annie Mae, talk to her in the most gentlesome way. With the money Mr. Hampton brought, her father did buy a Ford red belly tractor, but the rest was placed in the bank for the child. It made Naomi wonder how different he would have been as a father to her and Lila if their mother had lived longer. Learning people were so much more than you thought, wasn't that also part of no longer being a·child?

But if her father found out she was going to Jacob's grave . . . On Saturday, Annie Mae was getting her picture taken in Pulaski. Lila would drive them there. She'd tell her sister then. Lila wouldn't want Naomi going either, but she'd make Lila understand that it had to be done.

26

*D*ESIRE. *Jacob thought that too died with Naomi. For months it had, but not now. At Holder's Soda Shop, Veronica would twist the stool to talk to a girlfriend, her thigh brush against his and he'd feel the soft shock of firm flesh beneath the thin summer cloth, the touch of her fingertips across his arm. Last Saturday night at the VFW, she'd pressed the fullness of her breasts against him, her breath warm on his neck. Later, as they went to the parking lot, she said it was such a pretty night that they should go up to the Rock, walk around a bit, talk. We haven't had much chance to do that with everyone else around, she said. They had been there together before, kissing, caressing, but always with the understanding she wouldn't let it go beyond that. He and Veronica hadn't kissed since his return, but she made clear once they did there'd be no holding back.*

Jacob had told her he was tired and taken her home. Afterward, though, he hadn't gone back to Laurel Fork but instead to Price Lake. Jacob thought a few cars might be there, couples necking, some more than that, but the parking lot was empty. He left the truck and walked to the shore. Dark trees huddled around the banks. On the lake's still center, a crescent moon's emptycradle reflection. Less than a year ago, they'd decided to have a child. Naomi wanted it conceived beside water, not a lake but what she'd called quick water. In the sunlight too, because all things needed sunlight to grow. A superstition, but Naomi insisted. They'd taken a quilt to the far side of this lake where a stream entered. For three weekends in a row, they'd lain beside the stream, hearing the water, Naomi sometimes touching its surface as their bodies merged. Jacob had recalled these moments last Saturday night. There on Price Lake's dark shore, Jacob closed his eyes and remembered the feel of Naomi's body. Afterward, desire dimmed, he'd driven back to Laurel Fork.

Now though, as Ginny Watson placed her items on the counter, Jacob thought of how close he'd come to saying yes to Veronica's suggestion they be alone. Something else to feel bad about, like having to be reminded he and Naomi met on this day. As soon as Ginny left, Jacob called Agnes Dillard and ordered a spray of two dozen roses for Naomi's grave, a rose for each month. She promised to bring the flowers by midafternoon. For the rest of the day, Jacob thought about the marigolds, concluded that Blackburn was probably right. If the Clarkes wanted to hurt him, a spiteful letter or telegram would be the likelier way. Of course, the real hurt was others remembering what he himself had forgotten.

Come evening when Jacob walked up the drive, Blackburn didn't wait on the porch. Besides this morning's tiff, things hadn't been good between them of late, especially after Blackburn spoke of the heart's capabilities and Jacob's thickheaded response. He needed to patch things up. Maybe they could go fishing soon. It had been a good while since they'd done that.

He opened the cemetery gate and walked in. The roses lay like a bright blanket across the grave's center. Beside the spray, Blackburn's urn of orange flowers and the vase of marigolds. As the day's light waned, Jacob thought of two years ago in Blowing Rock, how by this time he and Naomi would have been in the theater, side by side in the darkness.

Jacob touched the stone, let his fingers pass over the marble as he thought of their wedding night, the smoothness of Naomi's skin, its warmth. But he also recalled cross words, moments of thoughtlessness never to be righted. Jacob thought about their last night together, how after they'd untwined, he lay with his arm around her, listening to Naomi breathe. Jacob might have slept if he'd tried, but asleep he wouldn't know he was with her, holding her. He'd believed that if he listened to every breath, dawn would come slower.

In San Diego harbor, as the last ropes slackened and the gangplank lifted, he'd looked out at the ocean and wondered how any ship could find its way in such vastness. Now Jacob looked around him at the cemetery, beyond it to the cottage. He was alone. In five more weeks, his and Naomi's second wedding anniversary would come. His parents had already spoken of the date as a signal for another point of departure. Jacob placed his hand on Naomi's stone, as if a buoy that might keep him from being swept away.

His parents were in bed when Jacob entered the house. He washed up, then went into the kitchen and poured a glass of water. He took a pill from the prescription bottle, hesitated, shook out a second. His mother came from her bedroom, cinching the cloth belt of her robe. She saw the two pills.

"Something troubling you, son?"

Jacob hesitated, then spoke.

"Blackburn came by the store today. Someone in Tennessee had Agnes Dillard deliver flowers for Naomi's grave."

"Flowers?" his mother asked, her hand tightening the robe against her neck. "Who sent them?"

"The note wasn't signed but Blackburn thinks Naomi's sister did it."

"They're in Michigan."

"Maybe they came back."

"But they, well, they just couldn't," his mother said. "Mr. Clarke said they sold their land, son, as I told you."

Jacob had never seen his mother look so flustered. She couldn't know if the Clarkes had returned or not, just didn't want to believe they had. His parents wanted to erase Naomi's existence, even beyond her gravestone.

"Blackburn thinks Mr. Clarke wouldn't sell his land."

"Those flowers could have been sent from a cousin or a friend," his mother insisted.

"But you can't know that for certain."

His mother's eyes, which had avoided his, now did not.

"Why does *any* of this matter, son?"

"Because someone cared enough to do it. They remembered this is the day Naomi and I met. *They* remembered, Momma, and I didn't," Jacob said, his voice breaking. "If I try to forget or I try to remember, either way feels wrong."

His father's footsteps hurried up the hall.

"Is everything all right?" he asked, eyes blinking as he stepped into the kitchen's light.

"It's fine, Daniel," his mother replied. "Go on back to bed. I'll be there in a minute."

"You're sure?" he asked, looking first at her, then Jacob.

"Yes," his mother said. "Let me talk to Jacob alone."

His father nodded and went back down the hallway.

"If you visited the cemetery less," his mother said gently, "maybe every other week, it could help."

"I need to go to bed," Jacob said, about to place the pills in his mouth.

"One more thing first," his mother told him. "It is important and needs to be said."

Jacob waited.

"When your sisters died, I went up to their graves each morning for weeks. Then one day I asked myself, Who am I doing this for? Who is this helping? When they were alive, my love could do so much for them, but not afterward. So I quit going. That sounds harsh, son, but life is harsh. Loving people when they are alive, that's what matters."

So you'd have stopped loving me if I'd died in Korea, Jacob thought.

Perhaps it was the look on Jacob's face, but his mother sensed the thought.

"I didn't say I stopped loving them, son," his mother said. "I never have."

Back in his bedroom, Jacob turned on the light and waited for the pills to take effect. He wondered if his mother had made the right choice. Couldn't trying to stifle grief just keep it trapped inside you?

The next morning when he awoke, he found his father slumped in the armchair, snoring softly. Last night Jacob had again been trapped under the ice. His father had shaken him awake, told Jacob it was only a bad dream. Then his father sat down in the chair. *Go back to sleep, son,* he had said. *You're home, you're safe.*

27

O N THAT SPRING AFTERNOON five years ago, Gant's mother had come to the store and asked for the Hamptons' help. She'd heard Wilkie was retiring, and the caretaker position would be a perfect job for Blackburn. After the fall harvest, Mrs. Gant told Cora, she and Blackburn's father might join their daughter and her husband in Florida's orange groves. *I'm thinking it best for Blackburn to stay here where people's used to him and not have to deal with new folks,* Mrs. Gant had said. *It'll be up to Blackburn, of course, but he is sixteen and needs to get a job somewheres.* When Cora agreed to talk to Reverend Hunnicutt on Blackburn's behalf, his mother was relieved. *Please don't tell my husband,* she'd added before leaving. *He'd not like me meddling this way.* Although Reverend Hunnicutt had an older man in mind for the job, Cora and Daniel had overruled the minister. Now obviously a mistake, Cora knew on Monday morning as she and Daniel spoke at the kitchen table, voices soft despite Jacob having left for the store.

"I can tell Hunnicutt to fire Gant," Daniel said.

"I'll deal with Gant," Cora said. "To fire him outright could make Jacob suspicious."

"How suspicious do you think he is?"

"If you mean about the girl, none, but he thinks the Clarkes may be in Tennessee," Cora said. "I told him a cousin or friend could have sent the flowers."

Down the road, the sawmill whistle blew, but Daniel did not get up.

"It seems we can't stop having to lie," Cora said.

"I know," Daniel sighed.

"The baby's been born by now," Cora said. "I keep thinking that one day there will be a knock. I'll open the door and the child will be there."

"I can visit Clarke again," Daniel said, "jog his memory about what he can lose."

"But if this wasn't their doing," Cora replied, "it could start something. Even if we're right, they might demand more money, or get suspicious something more is at stake. A phone call to the store or her father showing up, and Jacob would know. There was no note with the flowers, so they didn't want us or anyone else realizing who sent them."

"They really could have moved or are about to," Daniel said. "The baby's likely old enough now, and the money would give them a good start elsewhere. The flowers might be a way of saying good-bye."

Cora wondered how much Daniel believed his own words. She knew he was trying to bolster her. She remembered the girls, both lost when so many other children, some never taken to a hospital, survived the influenza. *We're owed.* Cora wanted to look toward the sky and scream the words. For months she had imagined the Tennessee–North Carolina boundary as a huge wall separating the two states. But now the wall had cracks for the truth to slip through.

"If it happens again, we'll have to risk confronting the Clarkes," Cora said. She raised a hand to rub her forehead, let her eyes close a few moments before continuing. "And what of Parson? He still hasn't come to the store. What we had him do, it weighs on him."

"He got himself involved by bringing us the telegram."

"I worry he might feel the need to unburden himself," Cora said.

"I know," Daniel said, meeting her eyes, "but if the worst happens, we wouldn't have even had Jacob these last months. He'd have come back from Korea and soon as possible moved away. That's what that girl swore would happen. Even if he was to find out the truth tomorrow, we've had the chance to show him how much we care about him," Daniel's voice catching. "Whatever else, he has seen it."

Cora nodded. They *had* shown their love, bared it in front of their son in a way they'd never done before. Even if he did find out tomorrow, and hated them for what they'd done, he had witnessed that love every day and night since he'd returned.

The whistle blew again and Daniel stood.

"I'll come down to the mill later to tally the freight estimates and order the new planer," Cora said, and Daniel nodded.

"Soon enough that girl will be married again," he said. "I bet she's already honing in on a new husband, and quick to find one with the dowry we gave her. Money's the only reason she married Jacob anyway."

But as Daniel reached for his hat and keys, Cora knew that was not true. Last week when she passed Jacob's room, she'd paused, then gone in and opened the drawer where he kept the letters. *You'll regret doing this,* Cora had told herself, but did it anyway. The letters were more literate than she'd expected, and deeper in feeling. As Cora placed the last one back in its envelope and closed the desk drawer, violating her son's privacy was the lesser regret. Whatever else might be said against Naomi, she had loved their son.

Things could yet work out. They really could. Jacob hadn't mentioned the Clarkes or the flowers yesterday. He'd eaten well, seemed in good spirits. Though tightlipped about it, Jacob was spending time with Veronica. Now that Jacob's farmhouse had been sold, they could start building a new one in the pasture, as they'd always planned. But Gant had to be dealt with, and harshly.

Cora waited until midmorning to walk up the hill. In those first years after the deaths of Mary and Isabelle, Daniel alone placed flowers on the graves each birthday, Christmas, and Easter. She knew others thought her refusal coldhearted. Perhaps at moments Daniel had too. After three years he stopped such acknowledgments. The graves had remained bare ever since. If Daniel sometimes went and stood before the markers, Cora did not know. But didn't the marble's neatly chiseled letters evoke an orderliness that belied the *wrongness* of their children's deaths? She, not Daniel, had told Greene no first names or dates be etched in the stones. No lambs or angels placed upon them.

At the cemetery, Gant was on one knee clipping grass around the fence. As Cora stepped closer, he set the clippers down and stood.

"I've come to see if you truly care about my son," Cora said.

Gant waited. He was a big man. You could forget that because he so often tried to make himself less noticeable.

"Those flowers," Cora said. "What makes you think the girl's family sent them?"

"The date and them being marigolds," Gant answered, not flinching from her gaze, voice terse. "The postmark said Pulaski, Tennessee. That's near where the Clarkes' farms are."

"You mean where the Clarkes *were*," Cora said. "And that note wasn't signed, so anyone could have sent those flowers."

"I think her sister sent them," Blackburn said flatly, then, almost as if thinking he could dismiss her, turned to pick up the clippers.

Cora stepped forward, set her foot on the blades.

"I'm not through talking. All I asked the last time I came up here was to let us heal our son the way we know best. That's all we asked, the kindness of that, the consideration." Cora paused. Blackburn faced her now but would not meet her eyes. "The only reason you got the caretaker's job is because of Daniel and me. Hunnicutt had someone else in mind, but your mother asked us to intervene. You didn't know that, did you? The point being we can also fire you. So here's what I can promise, Gant. If you try to talk Jacob into contacting the

Clarkes or try to yourself, you will be out of that cottage by nightfall. If flowers show up for that grave again, or anyone comes to it in person, you tell Daniel and me first. We'll decide what Jacob needs to know. Do you understand?"

Gant nodded.

"No, don't just nod," Cora said. "Tell me out loud that you understand."

"I understand."

Cora turned away. As she walked past the cemetery railing, she did not look within. Cora's eyes remained fixed on what was straight ahead of her.

28

BLACKBURN CHECKED the midmorning sky, found it cloudless. A thunderstorm might come but not before late afternoon, so he set the ladder against the eave, carried up the drop cloth, paint, and brushes, positioned them on the steeple base. His right side bore a purple bruise from the fight, sore but no cracked ribs. He unsealed a paint can, stirred the paint. Before starting Blackburn looked down at the spray of roses. It lay like a gaudy saddle over the grave, made the vase and urn like an afterthought. Yet it was Jacob who'd forgotten Saturday's significance. Perhaps there was a dance this weekend he'd take Veronica to. If not, they'd be together at Holder's Soda Shop.

Blackburn picked up a brush. The steeple was eight feet tall, so to reach the tip he'd have to balance both feet on the base corners, his free hand on the steeple. *You look down into enough holes,* Wilkie once told him, *you hardly notice much of the world above you.* In the past, whenever Blackburn looked beyond the spire's narrowing and into the sky, he'd always grown unsteady, so now as he dipped and swabbed, Blackburn kept his gaze level, the brush hairs blindly seeking the spire's tip. Soon what he painted was directly in front of him, his feet balanced on the roof comb. The spire was thicker now, so he twisted his body to coat the other side. The sun fell full upon him and he sweated. A shadow crossed the spire. Then the bird, a red-tailed hawk, glided past so close Blackburn saw the brown eye, the white feathers' dark banding. The hawk curved toward the church and veered upward. As it did, Blackburn's eyes followed. The spire began to spin. It was as if he was suddenly upside down, about to plummet into the blue emptiness. Blackburn dropped the brush and reached out, clung to the steeple with both arms. It might have been seconds or minutes, but the spinning finally stopped. Blackburn opened his eyes. The steeple and belfry, the church and the land around it, stabilized.

When his hands quit shaking, Blackburn picked up the brush and finished. Using a smaller brush, he touched up the belfry's bell slats, the belfry itself. He was almost done when Blackburn heard his name called.

"I saw you up there and figured you could use something cold," Jacob said, coming up the drive with two 7UPs in his hands.

"I ain't finished yet," Blackburn answered, and turned back.

"I'll stick around a few minutes," Jacob said, sitting on the steps. "It would be good to have someone steady that ladder when you come down."

"Might be more than a few minutes."

"That's all right," Jacob said, then waited until Blackburn had finished.

After holding the ladder, Jacob insisted on helping carry the equipment to the shed.

"Let me go in and get a nickel for that," Blackburn said when Jacob offered the 7UP.

"C'mon, Blackburn," Jacob said. "I know I acted like a jackass the other day. Please, let's sit down and drink these while they're cold."

Blackburn accepted the bottle and they sat. He took a long swallow, felt the coolness sliding down his throat, enjoyed the lingering sweetness.

"I'm of a mind it'll cool off some in a few days," Jacob said. "I'd like to get back to fishing again. I'm hoping you'll go with me. We haven't done that in a long while. Too long."

Blackburn gave only a shrug but it seemed to satisfy Jacob. They finished the drinks but Jacob didn't get up. He touched the ring on his left hand, his index finger sliding across the metal.

"I asked Momma at supper if they left Naomi's ring on her hand. They would have, wouldn't they?"

"I'd think so," Blackburn answered.

"Wasn't worth but a few dollars," Jacob said, looking out at the cemetery. "I was going to buy her a nice diamond when I got back from Korea. The day we eloped we did everything so quick it's like we never quite caught up."

Jacob's eyes remained on the cemetery.

"Naomi's ring," he said. "The reason I was thinking about it was because last night I dreamed I was back on that river. Beneath the ice I saw someone with long black hair. I thought it was a man at first, but then I saw the ring and knew it was

Naomi. She was holding something. . . . It was our baby, Blackburn."

Blackburn kept his eyes straight ahead, did not move even when Jacob picked up the bottles and stood. A single cicada, newly emerged, buzzed in the white oak. More would arise in the coming days, so many it would seem every leaf in the woods was charged with a current.

"I'm going to have to make some choices." Jacob sighed.

"What sort of choices?"

"About staying around here or leaving. Whether I can move on with my life the way my parents and damn near everyone else expects me to. This morning Momma mentioned building me a house in the pasture, like they've always wanted."

"What'd you say?"

"I didn't answer," Jacob said. "I'm not deciding something like that yet. I'll think it out hard. Knowing what's best, what's right, it isn't easy."

After Jacob left, Blackburn went to the springhouse. The oak-plank door creaked as he stepped into the darkness and after-rain smell. He lifted corn bread crumbs from his bib pocket, dropped them into the concrete trough. The trout took a crumb off the surface as it would a mayfly. Blackburn sat on a corner of the trough, let the springhouse's coolness dry the sweat. He thought about the day he had touched Naomi's stomach, felt the baby move.

Blackburn went back out, paused to let his eyes readjust. He still needed to wax the floors for next Sunday's homecoming, but at least the painting was done. Jacob spoke of decisions, but hadn't he been making one each time he let more days lapse between his cemetery visits? Before Mrs. Hampton's threat, Blackburn had pondered borrowing Reverend Hunnicutt's car and driving to Tennessee. No longer. To have to find work elsewhere, to approach strangers, endure the stares and flinches, that would be hard but doable. But to risk leaving Naomi here alone? No, he couldn't do that. Wherever the Clarkes were, Blackburn would not be the one to find them.

29

Aftter a day of dealing with patients, Dr. Egan needed solitude, so he always brought a book when he ate supper at Stuckey's Café. As soon as he sat down, he'd open it and pretend to read intently. Out of simple courtesy, most people wouldn't interrupt him. Others noted the book was often a medical treatise. Dr. Egan liked to imagine such people thinking *Best not to disturb the old fellow. What he's learning might someday save my life.*

Because it was Friday, the café would be busy, so Egan waited until seven-thirty before perusing his bookshelves and choosing *Human Anatomy.*

As he was about to leave, he saw a note on the desk.

Matt Goins asked what WE'D be doing after the practice closed. I told him that I am hitched to you only at the office.

A year after Helen died, Dr. Egan had received a similar response when he asked Ruthie to dinner. She had looked at him wryly. "Don't you think me putting up with you all day in here is effort enough?" Then her voice had softened. "There might have been a time I'd have said yes, but your eyes were on Miss Helen in her slinky dress and high heels, not me in my starched uniform and white crepe clodhoppers. I didn't have a chance." Ruthie had placed her palm on the back of Egan's hand, longer than a mere pat, but not lingering either—a confirmation and, as with Catherine, a pact. In both instances, a mature, sensible decision, yet there were times when he wished it otherwise, that he feared in such acquiescence too much had been conceded.

Egan set the note back on his desk. He turned off the light, locked the front door, and crossed the street. The sidewalks were less crowded now that midsummer had passed, but there was a line at the Yonahlossee, on the marquee *Strangers on a Train* in red plastic letters. Ben Parson was in the back of the line with his wife. As Dr. Egan neared, the telegraph operator turned his face away. Perhaps embarrassed about his request last March for sleeping pills. Men were easily shamed by something like that.

Approaching the soda shop, he contemplated a cup of ice cream for dessert. He looked inside the wide window. The booths and stools were filled and others stood awaiting service. The crowd might thin by the time he'd eaten. If not, he and Catherine could have ice cream on Sunday. He was about to go on when he saw Jacob Hampton on a stool near the back, Veronica Weaver beside him.

So his parents' child after all, Egan thought. A young man capable of moving on, of accepting doing so as his due. But that was being ungenerous. When Blackburn Gant had brought Jacob to his house that night in early June, Jacob had likely been shell-shocked, yet even then grief was evident. All summer, even as the war trauma lessened, Jacob's previously unfocused eyes revealed sorrow. But summer's lassitude would soon be on the wane. Autumn, like spring, brought forth a quickening, perhaps for Jacob too.

Daniel and Cora might finally have what they'd wanted all along, what the Weavers wanted too. But as Egan lingered at the window, he saw that Jacob wasn't dancing or laughing like the others. Once a month, Paul Moore continued to fill Jacob's Tuinal prescription, and when Dr. Egan checked his shoulder in late June, Jacob had been polite but distant. No, not healed completely. Yet how would he himself have continued life if Helen had died in 1918? At the time, he'd not have believed he could continue, but he surely would have.

When Dr. Egan entered the café, the back booth he preferred was occupied, so he took the front one and laid the book before him. Calvin Stuckey brought water and took his order. Though Egan preferred the seat opposite to be vacant, there were welcome exceptions, especially Paul Moore, who now entered the café.

"I'll have yours in a minute, Mr. Moore," the proprietor said.

"Join me while you're waiting, Paul," Egan said. "You hover above me like some ill angel."

The pharmacist sat down.

"Is it matters of the flesh or of the soul that you ponder tonight?" Moore asked, nodding at the book.

Egan gave the book a dismissive wave.

"Musings on the vagaries of love, so I suppose both."

"Alas, they do too often merge. Life would be easier if they didn't but also less interesting. Troubles with Miss Catherine?"

"No, just in a philosophical frame of mind."

"A bit melancholic then. My prescription is more Shakespeare and less Keats, that and two drams of Armagnac brandy."

Calvin Stuckey came from around the counter and handed Moore his order.

"Adieu, Doctor," Moore said as he stood. "You might recall fair Rosalind's words: 'Men have died from time to time, but not for love.'"

When he'd finished eating, Dr. Egan walked up the sidewalk. Holder's Soda Shop was still crowded. In the back, Jacob sat on the same stool, Veronica Weaver still beside him.

"*Te absolvo*," he whispered.

{ V }

30

I N THE TREES the season's last cicadas sang. Their hulls, nearly weightless, had littered the back of the cemetery for weeks. Now the insects themselves fell. Their bodies had a prettiness to them—all green at one moment, then tinged silver or blue if you turned them. Sometimes they lived a decade underground before emerging, or so some people claimed. Yesterday, Blackburn had walked down to the Ledfords' homeplace and found the Galas ripe. He liked how apples arrived at different times. Sweet Galas first, tart Granny Smiths last. Some apples had already fallen. Wasps and yellow jackets clung to the bruised fruit. The two apples Blackburn picked had been just right, the satisfying crunch, the white gleam inside bright as their taste. He'd always enjoyed this time of year, like the world was wanting to be especially generous before cold weather's hardships. A few more warm days and the air would cool, cleansed of summer's haze.

Blackburn finished raking and looked down at the store. Jacob's cemetery visits were only on Wednesdays and Sundays now, though he'd made an exception for August 23, Naomi's birthday. After each visit, Blackburn and Jacob still sat on the porch afterward, but their talk about Naomi was more guarded, like poker players hiding their cards. Since Mrs. Hampton's threat, Blackburn hadn't said a word about the Clarkes. Jacob hadn't mentioned them either. On Naomi's birthday, Agnes Dillard brought no marigolds for the grave, so perhaps the Clarkes, wherever they were, chose to turn their thoughts to the living. Yet Blackburn couldn't believe they, or at least Lila, wouldn't one day come.

At midafternoon, Robert Greene's truck came up the drive, bringing a stone for Alexander Pettigrew's grave. After the trench was dug, Blackburn helped slide the stone off the bed.

"It's a heavy one," Mr. Greene said. "You reckon the two of us can carry it?"

"We can try," Blackburn answered.

Twice the mason nearly lost his grip, Blackburn lowering his arms to tilt the weight toward himself. The stone set in place, Mr. Greene wiped his brow with a handkerchief.

"You're ever a strong man, Gant," he said, and grinned. "Too bad them boys at the pool hall didn't come to me so I could have warned them."

Mr. Greene knelt and patted the ground around the marker, got up and appraised the stone.

"Pettigrew's daughters said both names had to be on one line. Wouldn't have it no other way since their mother's is so. The spacing's skinny but I think it come out all right. Up north, lots of them folks got given and family names that wind out ten or twelve letters apiece. I bet them masons have a chore with that."

"You done good," Blackburn said, studying the chiseling.

Atop the stone's base, the tympanum's round center and two side caps were especially well done. Blackburn remembered drawing one for Naomi. She'd said it looked like an old woman pulling a shawl onto her shoulders. It did seem so. As they walked out the gate, Blackburn asked if the mason was going back to Blowing Rock.

"You need a ride in?"

"Yes, I need to pick up a glass pane," Blackburn said, "that and a new regulator for the church furnace."

"It is getting to be that time of year," Mr. Greene said. "Let's go."

As they passed Hampton's Store the mason asked how Blackburn thought Jacob was doing.

"Better."

"I'm glad to hear that," Greene said. "He's been through a lot. His parents have been too."

When Blackburn didn't respond, the older man quit talking.

Greene let him out in front of Weaver's Hardware, on the door WILL BE CLOSED MONDAY FOR LABOR DAY. Blackburn hadn't been back in Blowing Rock but once since the fight. Billy's truck was parked in front of Magill's Pool Hall, but if Troy or Billy saw him they'd not be inviting Blackburn in again. It was a new feeling to have people scared of something besides his face.

Blackburn stepped into the hardware store. Mr. Weaver

stood at the counter and nodded warily. At the back, Veronica placed orange price tags on rakes, so Blackburn hurried and found the pane and regulator. Before he could pay though, Veronica joined him, asked how he thought Jacob was doing.

"Better," Blackburn replied.

Veronica spoke, softer this time.

"I guess he still comes up to the cemetery often."

Blackburn wanted to sidle past her but the aisle was narrow. He felt a sudden anger.

"Not much as he used to."

Veronica's chin lifted. The concern on her face was there, but for a moment it lessened. She looked down in a shy way, tucked a strand of hair behind her ear.

"I need to go," Blackburn said, brushing past her.

She followed him to the counter.

"I can give you a ride," Veronica offered as her father wrote up the purchases. "I planned on going by the store today, just to say hi to Jacob and ask about dinner. That would be okay, wouldn't it, Dad?"

"Take your time," Mr. Weaver said. "If you see Cora or Daniel, tell them hello for me."

"I have other doings in town," Blackburn said and left, but Veronica followed him onto the sidewalk.

"Does Jacob ever mention me?"

"Sometimes."

When she asked if Jacob said nice things, Blackburn nodded.

"Good," Veronica said when he offered nothing more. "There's something else I wanted to ask you."

Blackburn waited.

"I've heard her family's never come to visit," Veronica said. "Is that true?"

"I got to go," Blackburn said, and crossed the street.

After Veronica drove off, Blackburn started the walk back home. He passed Magill's Pool Hall, but Billy's truck was gone.

Come evening, the furnace regulator and windowpane replaced, Blackburn sat on the porch. With fewer cicadas, sounds drowned out for weeks reemerged. Soon frost would silence the frogs and crickets too, send the warblers south. The owls would remain, calling even on the coldest nights. It being Wednesday, Jacob soon came up the drive. His steps now were more stride than shuffle, purposeful. He didn't smile as much as before Korea and his eyes lacked the spark they'd once had, but those things might yet return. Jacob nodded to Blackburn and went on into the cemetery. As always, he stood head down, hands clasped before him. Whether Jacob's eyes were closed, whether his lips moved, Blackburn never could tell.

As he waited on the porch, Blackburn wondered if he'd caused Billy Runyon to leave the pool hall. Even so, he knew Billy wasn't through with him. Come Halloween night, he'd not be surprised if Billy showed back up at the cottage. He'd keep the car or truck doors locked, not get out, but lean on the horn, crack a window to shout. Blackburn thought how close he came to ripping Billy's face open. In his childhood before the polio struck him, Blackburn had been an obedient son. He'd never bullied anyone or been cruel that he could remember. But he'd done much of his growing later than most boys. If the polio hadn't happened, might he be more like Billy?

Blackburn's thoughts turned, as they'd often done these last six weeks, to what his mother had requested of Jacob's parents. Doing what was best for *Blackburn,* his mother had told Mrs. Hampton. Best for *him,* just as her finding a reason to take only Blackburn's sister with her when she went to town.

Jacob left the cemetery and sat down on the steps.

"We finally signed over the deed to the farmhouse and you can bet I'll never go near it again," Jacob said. "I'm hurting enough as it is."

Blackburn wasn't certain that was true, but then Jacob spoke again.

"Momma and Daddy, people in the store and at the ice cream shop, none of them mention Naomi. You and me, Blackburn, we're the only ones who do."

After Jacob walked down the drive, Blackburn sat awhile longer, trying to settle his mind. The weathervane creaked. Change was coming.

31

Y OU'VE GOT *to move on with your life, Lila had said four weeks ago, not just for yourself but Annie Mae. Daddy can look after a passel of sleeping children good as you can. Ansel will be at the dance and I want you to meet him. He's hardworking and easy to get along with.*

Is Ansel a man or a mule?

You best listen to me, sister, Lila bristled. Daddy's near wore out. You'll need a man to help keep a roof over you and that young one's head.

All right then, I'll meet him, Naomi had agreed, but not before I go and tell Jacob good-bye.

You can't do that. You'll be seen and lose your daughter.

I'll go late at night.

It's still too much a risk.

I'll go whether you help me or not. I'll take a bus, walk the rest of the way. You know I'll do it.

There ain't no way Daddy—

He won't know, Naomi replied, if you help me.

Now, the anniversary was only days away. The clothing

from the Sears wish book had arrived at Lila's house, the photograph taken in Pulaski placed in an oval glass frame. Lila was still trying to talk her out of going. And not only because of the risk to Annie Mae. Lila also believed Naomi's brief marriage had offered only a glimpse of love, not the deep, abiding kind that took years. Yet Lila was right about soon needing another hand on the farm. Their father was wearing down—lumbago, swollen fingers, not near as strong as he'd once been. The Hamptons' money would help for a while, but only awhile. For the last two weeks Naomi hadn't opened her schoolbooks. Annie Mae had been colicky, but that wasn't the real reason. Naomi was tired of dreaming. Hadn't life taught her how frail dreams were, so quickly shattered? If she could talk to Blackburn, he might help her figure things out. *If he cared about you, he'd have shown up by now*, Lila had told her. And yet . . . Blackburn had loved Jacob same as her. He'd never say that word out loud, but it was true nevertheless. If Blackburn knew about Annie Mae, he'd love her also.

The black dress and its tulle were at Lila's house. A marriage with no wedding dress, only widow's weeds. Worn one night, then put away. Lila said the money was better spent on Annie Mae, but Naomi didn't agree. Blackburn believed the cemetery's dead were aware of such gestures. Every stitch of black cloth would show Jacob the whelming of what was inside her.

Her father in the field and Annie Mae asleep, Naomi turned the photograph over to the ragwood backing, wrote the words she would leave with Jacob, printing each letter and number carefully before hiding the oval frame beneath the quilts that awaited winter. Naomi sat down on the bed. She'd always known life could be hard. If you had faith, maybe there'd come a time, as the hymn said, when there'd be nary a sorrow nor care, but shouldn't this life have its share of joy too? Or was that just more childishness? Lila was wrong about Naomi only glimpsing love. The heart's full knowing came only with loss. Lila didn't understand that. If she was lucky, she might never have to.

32

O N NAOMI AND JACOB'S wedding anniversary, as on July 28, Blackburn awoke to the sound of rain. He dressed and ate. Feeling restless, he went into the church and polished the pews with linseed oil. The sanctuary was chilly. For the first time since March, the furnace might be needed. Wanting something else to do, he went to the shed and used a mill file to sharpen the mower blades. Agnes Dillard had brought no flowers on Naomi's birthday, but Blackburn wondered if she might today. He couldn't shake the inkling that something was about to happen, even as the morning passed undisturbed.

Late afternoon, the rain softened into a misty drizzle. Below the springhouse, Blackburn gathered the season's last cardinal flowers. Tall and bright red, they were easy to find this time of year. He went to the cemetery and replaced the flowers in the urn. The storm had shaken branches off the white oak. Blackburn picked them up, including one on Shay Leary's grave. The weathervane shifted. Clearer skies were coming.

Blackburn was finishing an early supper when he heard the iron gate open. Through the window he saw Jacob, before him a blush of red, moving toward the cemetery's center. Blackburn went and stood on the porch. Despite the mist and chill, Jacob stayed as the gray day thickened into darkness. Blackburn went inside and boiled a pot of coffee. The night's dampness seeped into the cottage. He'd built a couple of hearth fires during a cool spell in June but hadn't restocked the fire box. All that remained were a few logs of pine. They would have to do. Blackburn tucked newspaper and kindling under them and struck a match. When the logs caught, their flames bloomed yellow.

At last the flashlight switched on, its beam like a cane guiding Jacob back through the stones. Blackburn stepped onto the porch. At the cemetery entrance, Jacob stopped, hand on the gate. It remained there. Then, ever so slowly, he wedged the hinge onto the latch. As Jacob came closer, Blackburn saw he wore no hat or jacket. His shirt and pants were soggy, hair matted, lips tinged blue.

"You need to come inside and dry out," Blackburn said, stepping off the porch. "I got coffee made and a fire going."

For a few moments the only sound was water dripping off the cottage's eaves.

"The right kind of weather for today," Jacob said softly.

"Yes, it is," Blackburn agreed.

Jacob shivered, turned his head toward the cemetery as if he might go back.

"You got to come in and get warm," Blackburn said.

Jacob didn't move until Blackburn took his elbow.

"Come on."

Inside, they stood before the hearth, sipping coffee but not speaking. How many words had been spoken within these walls? Blackburn wondered. From what he knew, not many during Wilkie's tenure. In his own, except for the winter when he and Jacob were seventeen, hardly any. In a room anywhere else, his and Jacob's continued silence might be awkward, but here it felt natural. The pine burned quick. By the time they emptied their cups, last embers glowed amid gray ash, but Jacob no longer shivered, his clothes nearly dry.

"Thank you," Jacob said softly, setting the cup on the table.

Blackburn followed him outside. After Jacob disappeared down the drive, Blackburn went to confirm what Jacob had brought. Set beside the urn was a green vase holding a dozen roses. Like the cardinal flowers Blackburn had placed in the urn, the roses were red. Blackburn remembered the pale sarvisberry flowers he'd placed here in March. At least some brightness.

Returning to the cottage, Blackburn took the playing cards off the fireboard and set the deck on the table. For a few minutes he left the cards untouched, instead drank a second and third cup of coffee as he stared out the window. The mist had lifted, even a few stars peeking through. Blackburn thought of Shay Leary, at peace now, and those on Brown Mountain who were not. His mind turned to Wilkie, the man who'd given Shay Leary that peace. Blackburn wondered if Wilkie was still alive. The old man had come back only once, four years ago. He and Blackburn had walked through the cemetery together. Wilkie said that town life wasn't so different from here. Yes, folks were bustling about, but they didn't have time to notice you. *I waited too long to leave,* Wilkie told him.

In another hour, the room grew chilly. Then it was eleven, his bedtime, but Blackburn reshuffled the cards, spread the seven columns on the table, and began another game. Half an hour later, Blackburn heard a soft clink. At the cemetery's entrance a light appeared, disappeared, then reappeared before drifting through the stones. At the cemetery's center, the light paused but did not expire. *Jacob,* he thought, because no headlights had come up the drive. Perhaps to say something unsaid earlier or just to be with Naomi. Maybe even, as others secretly had, to place a keepsake, a ring, on Naomi's grave as a final good-bye to her, to their marriage.

Blackburn went out on the porch and down the steps. Now he saw that, unlike a flashlight's steady beam, the light flickered. A lantern. Its glow outlined the nearby headstones. Blackburn crossed the parking lot and stopped at the cemetery entrance. There were eight rows between the gate and Naomi's grave, but he could see the lantern on the mound. The globed flame's motion made the stone's one word tremble, the fylfot appear to slowly spin.

Only then did Blackburn realize it might be a trick played by Billy or, even worse, a desecration. He could have parked on the roadside to sneak up here. Now, though partly hidden by another stone, something shifted beside the lantern. Blackburn looked harder. An outline began to emerge of a presence darker than the night itself. He heard a whisper, but no one answered in response. Moments passed. Then from the heart of the graveyard came the sound of weeping.

The gate was open. *Inviting me in,* Blackburn thought. He passed through the gate, felt the slick grass beneath his boots. He stepped quietly, stopped halfway where he could see without obstruction. The lantern's light revealed a woman's silhouette, her back turned to Blackburn. She wore a black funeral dress and a mourning veil. The tulle was swept back, tucked behind her ears like silky wings. He could not see her hands or face. Blackburn took another step forward. The mourner turned and Blackburn saw the face of a woman come to grieve at her own grave.

As the tulle resettled, an arm reached out toward him. To implore or to accuse, Blackburn did not know. He took a step and his right boot hit a foot marker. He fell sideways and his head hit something hard. Stars swirled and pulsed like sparks in an updraft. As his eyes closed, a voice whispered his name. Blackburn felt a webby softness brush over his face and he heard his name again. Then he was drifting and all was silent.

When his eyes opened. Blackburn fixed his gaze on a single star, waiting for it to anchor the sky. The star finally steadied. He raised himself onto one knee. The urn and vase remained on the grave but the lantern and its bearer were gone. He walked unsteadily to the cottage, managed to get his boots off before falling back into darkness.

His waking the next morning came in blurry stages. Only a dream, Blackburn thought, and closed his eyes. The next time he awoke, he wasn't so sure. His head hurt. Dark blood stained the pillow. He touched the side of his head, felt an eggy swelling. When Blackburn set his feet on the floor, he grew dizzy. The pain came like anvil strikes. He went into the bathroom, poured a BC Powder into a cup of water and drank, returned to the cot and slept again.

By midmorning, the headache had lessened. He went to the bathroom, poured iodine on a washrag. Holding the poultice to his head, Blackburn walked into the front room and looked out the window. The rain and mist were gone, the sun angling in from the east. His and Jacob's flowers were still on Naomi's grave, situated exactly as they'd been yesterday. He removed the cloth, raised a finger and reconfirmed the swelling. How could he be certain of anything after a blow like this?

"I saw her," Blackburn said aloud. She'd turned and looked right at him. *You got to clear your head,* he told himself. Blackburn poured cold coffee into his cup and sat down, swallowed the liquid as he might an elixir. More memories rose as if lifted from murky water, including how the lantern shone on the stone's one word, a name incomplete, partially concealed just as Shay Leary's had once been.

Blackburn took the washrag to the bathroom and rinsed it, splashed water on his face. He came back and stared out the window. Sunlight filled the cemetery, made water beads sparkle. She had come to him, not Jacob, yet Jacob would have to be the one to add *Naomi* to the marker. And if Jacob refused? But what if she might have appeared for another reason? Blackburn hadn't noticed if Jacob wore the wedding ring when he'd left the cemetery. Could that be what Naomi mourned?

Before anything else, check the grave, he decided, and went outside. The gate was open, and Blackburn felt its being so had meaning. He stepped through. The urn and vase were exactly where they'd been placed, but as he looked more carefully, Blackburn saw a line of unsettled soil at the marker's base. He hesitated, then told himself he had to know. With his index finger, Blackburn probed the loose dirt. He felt something, but it wasn't Jacob's wedding ring. He worked the object free. An oval picture frame, small enough to fit in his palm. Blackburn brushed the glass and an infant's face appeared. He turned the frame over and rubbed dirt off the backing.

Annie Mae Hampton
Your Daughter

On the lower rim of the backing

Hudson Photography
Pulaski, Tennessee
August 1951

This cannot be real. That was Blackburn's first thought—not the words, but the object he held. Yet as his hand tightened, held it as if it might escape, Blackburn felt the frame's metal rim, the slow curve, the solidity. Felt the smooth glass on his palm. He opened his hand, read the words and date again. Blackburn turned the frame over, studied the infant's face. Naomi's child, a daughter. A question came, and with it the answer. The veil had been swept back only a moment. Just a glance. *As alike as two peas in a pod,* Naomi had said.

But Lila couldn't have walked here from Tennessee. Blackburn placed the picture frame in his front pocket and went down the drive. In the weeds by the roadside, he found fresh tire prints, a spent kitchen match. Mrs. Hampton lying to

Jacob about the Clarkes moving made sense now. The Clarkes mustn't want Jacob to know either. Else why come at night? Why hide the photo? Yet on the backing, the child's last name was Hampton. Why not hide that?

His child is alive, so cross the road and tell him. What then? One certainty, the Hamptons would see to it that Blackburn was fired. The simplest thing would be to place the picture back where he'd found it, only deeper, where it would never again come to light. Instead, Blackburn walked up the drive, not to the graveyard but to the manse.

"I got need to borrow your car," Blackburn said when Reverend Hunnicutt came to the door.

"That shouldn't be a problem," the minister answered. "I won't need it until a five o'clock visit. Does that suit?"

"No sir, I likely need it most of the night."

Reverend Hunnicutt frowned.

"I don't think I can lend it that long, Blackburn. Is this that important, something to do with your family?"

"Not my family," Blackburn said. "But it's important, real important."

"And needs to be done today?" the minister asked.

"Yes sir."

Reverend Hunnicutt looked toward the Studebaker, as if it might sway him one way or another.

"All right then," he said. "I'll call and put off my home visits until tomorrow. You'll be certain to return by morning?"

"Yes sir."

An hour later Blackburn neared the crest of Roan Mountain. Though his mind had cleared, every thought came like steps on a shaky bridge. Perhaps talking to the Clarkes might convince him that Jacob was better off *not* knowing about the child. Lila and her husband could raise it easier than Jacob alone, especially if Jacob decided to move away. Even if Jacob remained in Laurel Fork, Mr. and Mrs. Hampton had made clear to everyone how they felt about the child.

And what would Jacob feel? Would he, deep inside himself, wish he'd never known about her, especially if trying to leave past sorrows behind?

As Blackburn drove through Knoxville, he told himself he could still turn back, rebury the picture, and forget last night. But he kept driving west. Blackburn wondered if Naomi had held Annie Mae before she died, at least known the child would live. He hoped so. What would Naomi, the child's mother, think best? Even if it was having Lila and Hugh raise her, wouldn't Naomi want Jacob to know he had a daughter? *Just get there,* Blackburn told himself. *Soon enough you'll have more of a handle on it.*

Finally, the land began to level, then rose again, hills not mountains. He entered Pulaski, turned right. Blackburn found the Clarkes' farm easier this time. He parked and crossed over the creek. Naomi's father kneeled in the cabbage patch, his butcher knife sawing through a stalk. Blackburn did not see the child, but on the clothesline hippins hung alongside overalls.

Mr. Clarke did not raise a hand in greeting, and when he left the field and stepped into the yard he went toward the house. Leaning against the porch rail was the shotgun. He picked it up and turned, the gun barrel pointed at Blackburn's feet.

"You best head it back to North Carolina," he said, gesturing toward the car. "You and any you brought with you."

"I didn't bring nobody with me," Blackburn answered.

Naomi's father kept the shotgun pointed in Blackburn's direction.

"The baby," Blackburn said, nodding at the clothesline. "Where is she?"

"That's none of your damned business," Mr. Clarke answered, raising the barrel. "If you've come for that chap, or bringing some piece of paper that claims a sheriff or pettifogger aims to—"

"Nobody sent me," Blackburn said.

"You tell them Hamptons you was coming?"

"No sir."

"Or anyone else?"

"No."

Mr. Clarke glanced toward the car again.

"You swear it so?"

"Yes."

Mr. Clarke lowered the barrel. He leaned the shotgun against the porch rail, turned his gaze back to Blackburn.

"You being here, it's on account of seeing her last night?"

"Yes."

"I didn't know about any of that foolishness, thought Lila at least had sense enough to know better," he said, shaking his head. "I heard you fell and hit your head a hard lick."

"I did."

"If I'd just known, I'd have stopped her from going," Mr. Clarke said. "We'd all be better off."

Blackburn suspected it was true. He'd be at the cemetery, no confusion, his duties certain.

"Is Annie Mae at Lila's?"

"Why do you need to know?" Mr. Clarke asked, brow furrowing.

"I need to understand why you all and the Hamptons kept that child a secret," Blackburn answered.

"You're not seeing Naomi or that baby neither one, least-ways till I'm clear about what you got on your mind."

"Lila, you mean, not Naomi," Blackburn said, surprised at the older man's slip.

Mr. Clarke looked puzzled.

"I thought you just seen Naomi last night, not Lila too."

Blackburn studied the older man more closely. Age, grief, isolation—something had addled him.

"I know Naomi's dying has been hard," Blackburn said softly. "I miss her too."

"What in the hell are you talking about?" Mr. Clarke said. "The onliest one dead is her husband."

33

AFTER MORE WORDS, Blackburn and Mr. Clarke stared at each other with suspicion. Frustration too, deepening into anger.

"I buried Naomi myself," Blackburn said. "I dug the grave and covered up her coffin."

"You're lying about that boy being alive," the older man countered. "I'm thinking this ain't nothing but a trick to get Annie Mae."

He turned toward the house, but Blackburn grabbed his arm.

"You ain't pointing that shotgun at me again."

Mr. Clarke tried to jerk free.

"Let me go into the house and I'll by God show you proof he's dead."

"I got proof enough with my own two eyes," Blackburn said, tightening his grip on the older man's arm. "Jacob's at his parents' house down the hill from me. I see him near every day."

"Naomi was here this morning, come to tell what happened last night," Mr. Clarke said. "She seen that boy's grave, seen you. Hell, *you* seen her. That's why she and Annie Mae is at Lila's right now, scared you'd tell the Hamptons she'd broke the contract me and that boy's daddy made. And damn it, I still ain't sure they didn't send you."

Their faces were close now, but the older man did not avert his gaze.

"Let's see your 'proof,'" Blackburn said.

Inside, Mr. Clarke pointed at the fireboard. Beside schoolbooks and the wooden tractor was a telegram. Blackburn read it twice, reconfirmed the sender's name and address.

"I'm keeping that," the older man said, snatching the telegram from Blackburn.

"It ain't real."

"What you mean it ain't real? It says Western Union right there on it."

"How'd that telegram get delivered here?"

"That boy's father brought it," Mr. Clarke exclaimed, then after a few moments, "You're saying it's fake."

"That's right," Blackburn answered, but the older man seemed not to hear. "Now tell me why you're claiming Naomi's alive."

"Look around you," he said, nodding at Naomi's winter coat hung on a nail, schoolbooks on the fireboard. "Go in her room if you need more convincing."

Blackburn did so. The widow's weeds were folded neatly on the bed. He went over to the bureau, picked up a receipt from Sears, Roebuck dated August 16, Naomi's name on it, another receipt from Hudson Photography, August 12. One of the Blue Horse tablets he'd brought her was on the bureau.

Blackburn opened it, *May 23, 1951* in the upper right-hand corner. He read a few sentences, turned pages until he came to the last entry. *September 5.* Below, *Tonight I will tell your father all about you.*

Blackburn took the oval frame out of his pocket, compared the writing to that on the photograph's backing. He closed the tablet, set his hand on the bureau to steady himself. He thought about the magnitude of lies the Hamptons had told him. It was coming clear now, the coffin he'd not been allowed to carry, the way Murdock had stayed behind to see the grave filled. They'd lied to Dr. Egan and to their own son. Blackburn recalled the sound of dirt hitting the coffin, nights he'd spent beside the grave.

Blackburn went into the front room. Mr. Clarke stood by the fireboard, the toy tractor in his hand.

"That young'un loves watching these wheels roll. I hope it don't mean she's got the itch to travel, like her mother done." For the first time since Blackburn had arrived, the man's face softened. "But Annie Mae's ever a sweet little child."

"I got to see Naomi now."

"You come round to believing she's alive?" Mr. Clarke asked.

"Yes, but I still got to see her. There's so much I ain't got untangled." Blackburn took out his billfold, removed the newspaper clipping. "Here, if you still don't believe Jacob's alive."

Mr. Clarke glanced at the clipping, angrily handed it back.

"I should of figured when his son-of-a-bitch father offered that much money there was more to it, but as long as they stuck to their side of the state line I was glad to stay on mine."

"You believe me?" Blackburn asked.

"Yes, but you and me," Naomi's father said, "they's still something we need to talk out."

"We can do that later, damn it." Blackburn's headache had returned and everything his mind was trying to hold together felt about to collapse. "Please, I got to know that all of this, all of it . . . is real."

"Sit down," the older man said. Though the room was warm, he nodded toward two chairs before the hearth. "Rocking helps you think things out better."

"Please," Blackburn said again. "When I see Naomi I can tell her Jacob's alive. Then I can drive back and tell him so he will know the truth."

Mr. Clarke stared at Blackburn with as much incredulity as any time since his arrival.

"What makes you think I'd let any of them folks set foot near Annie Mae after all their lies and threats?"

"That was his parents. Once Jacob knows what happened he'll not let them near that child."

"So you claim," Mr. Clarke answered. "The apple don't fall far from the tree. That dear child's got kin here who care about her. Lila and Hugh and their young ones cherish every breath that girl takes. I do too. You said earlier he's living with his parents, him doing that knowing how they treated Naomi."

"Jacob was in real bad shape when he first come back," Blackburn said. "He needed their help. He still can't do a lot with the shoulder he hurt."

"Ain't never going to get better then," Naomi's father

asked, anger but also curiosity in his voice, "that shoulder, I mean?"

"No, but it don't stop him from running the store."

Outside, a whip-poor-will called, was answered. For the first time since they'd come into the house, Blackburn heard the creek's gurgle. As he'd learned evenings when he and Jacob sat on the porch steps, even the softest talk muffled so much else.

"Jacob don't have the least cause to think Annie Mae's alive?" Mr. Clarke asked.

"No," Blackburn answered. "They told him the same as me, that Naomi and the baby both died."

"If you care as much about Naomi as you claim, it's best you keep him believing that," Mr. Clarke said. He got up and lit the lamp on the kitchen table. "Night settles into this holler early. They's not time to get to Lila's place before dark."

"That car's got headlights."

"Them headlights need to know the right road to follow."

"Then you can take me," Blackburn snapped. "You best understand I ain't to be trifled with."

"I ain't to be trifled with neither," Mr. Clarke answered. "Naomi come here when she needed help and I give it to her and that baby. Not those damn Hamptons, nor Jacob, nor you. I took her in after she defied me and married that boy. Many a parent wouldn't have. So I'm the one decides who sees Naomi and who don't."

"Jacob knows where Lila's house is."

Mr. Clarke grimaced.

"You'd still go back and tell him she's alive, even after all we've just figured out about that family?" He reached out his hand, set it firmly on Blackburn's forearm. "I got something to say before you do that."

"Then tell it," Blackburn said. He flexed his forearm, but Mr. Clarke did not move his hand.

"You can stay."

"No," Blackburn answered. "I got to go."

"I ain't talking about tonight, son. You know how to farm. You're stout. I'm starting to flag some, but with you here we could make this farm prosper. Clear more land and plant more crops, buy a few more cattle, and we'd do fine."

"I got a job and place to live," Blackburn said.

"It don't come with a wife though, does it?"

Blackburn studied the man, searching for the least hint of amusement or cruelty, found none.

"If you settle in here with me, Naomi, and that baby, things will take their natural course. Husband material has got rare in these parts. Either they're in that war or off to Detroit to make cars. Naomi's got a fondness for you, and that face don't bother her none. Never mentioned it but to say that very thing. *His heart shines through it.* She said that about you. I'll nod Naomi in your direction too, though I doubt you'd need my help. Like I say, just let things take their natural course."

"You ain't got the right—"

"I got every right."

"You sound like the Hamptons."

"Then maybe for all their sorriness they taught me some things, especially about who belongs where." Mr. Clarke's eyes met Blackburn's. "Naomi told me about you being alone on that hill with nothing but dead folks for company. Jacob's a handsome enough fellow and will have the pickings of girls to court. Town girls, the kind his momma and daddy wanted him to marry, the sort that fits in better than Naomi ever could. Grieving does ease up. Like I said, Naomi was in a bad way after we got that telegram. Wouldn't do much more than lay in bed. But she's easing out of it. I'd have stopped her from going last night if I'd known about it ahead of time, but I can't misdoubt she had to say good-bye. She'll have no cause to go again. Leave things the way they are, son. I'm telling you it's best for everyone, including that child."

"Don't you owe Naomi—"

"I'm owed something too, damn it," Mr. Clarke said through clenched teeth. "I worn myself out to keep this farm going, keep a roof over her and Annie Mae's heads."

Blackburn got up, opened the door, stepped onto the porch but went no farther. In a few moments, the rocking chair resumed, soon steady as a ticking clock. Then the chair stopped.

"Come back in, son," Mr. Clarke said. "Stay the night and things will come clear to you tomorrow."

"I promised to have the car back by morning," Blackburn said. "You got to take me to Lila's now."

"Not tonight. You need some hours to think this thing out. You'll see I'm right about what's best . . . for everyone."

"You mean best for you," Blackburn answered, and stepped off the porch.

"Wait." Mr. Clarke sighed. He took the lantern off the nail, lit it, and joined Blackburn. "Whatever hard words I've said, they ain't aimed at you. You can be the best thing that's happened to this family. We got fifty acres here, but I'm only working twenty. You and me could double that. We'll give Naomi and what children come a good life." He raised the lantern higher as they came to the creek. "Here's something else to ponder. Think if you hadn't happened to look out and see her, you'd never knowed she and her baby was alive. Some folks would call that luck, but maybe it's more like things balancing out."

They passed over the bridge, their boot steps reverberating on the planks. Blackburn was about to get in the Studebaker but Mr. Clarke set a hand on the car door.

"I got a few more words before you leave, son. You think you'll get another chance to have what you could have here? A wife and daughter, soon enough more children? I ain't telling Naomi nothing about you coming today. You best think who you want to be with, them that's alive or them that's dead. I'm of a mind you've not had many choices in your life. You got one now."

As Blackburn drove toward North Carolina, he thought not of this night but a future one. In the hearth, flames ebb. Snow falls outside and wind gusts rattle windows as Annie Mae's breaths soften and the rocking chair stills. As Blackburn prods the logs with a poker, sets the fire screen in place, Naomi takes the child and lays her in the crib. Blackburn lifts the oil lamp and follows. He holds the light over the sleeping child, tucks the quilts closer around her, and places the lamp on the chest of drawers. He and Naomi change into their nightclothes. Blackburn turns the lamp's wheel and the room is dark. He lies down on the bed where Naomi awaits.

Don't think it. You're only going to hurt yourself more, Blackburn told himself, gripped the steering wheel harder and focused on the road. By the time he entered Knoxville, the gas gauge hovered near empty. He pulled into an Esso station. The man who came out wore an olive green field cap. While pumping the gas, he kept glancing at Blackburn's face, finally asked if he'd been wounded in Korea. Blackburn shook his head and paid.

As the road began to climb, Blackburn let his mind rein free. If he wore his coat and boots, all else he owned would fit in a duffel bag. He could pack tonight and write a note to Reverend Hunnicutt and leave it in the church. Come morning walk to the bus station and buy a ticket to Pulaski, from there a taxi to the farm. By tomorrow this time he could be with Naomi and Annie Mae.

At the top of Roan Mountain, the land drew back as if surrendering to the sky. Blackburn stopped at the overlook marking the state boundary. He got out and stretched his back. Not too much farther. It was very quiet. Leaves rustled, then stilled. Blackburn walked to the edge, before him an overspill of stars. They met his level gaze in each direction. No single look could even begin to contain them.

34

I T WAS 2:00 A.M. when he passed Hampton's Store and the house. Only Jacob's light was on. His parents, who deserved the worst sort of dreams, slept peacefully. Blackburn thought how easily he could wake them, the words he could say, but instead he went up the drive and parked in front of the manse. He had planned to slide the key beneath the door, but the porch light came on.

"I hope you were able to get your matter resolved," Reverend Hunnicutt said as he took the key.

"No sir, not yet."

"I'm sorry," the minister said. "If you want to talk about what's troubling you . . ."

"I appreciate the offering, but I got to figure it out for myself."

Reverend Hunnicutt nodded.

"If I had need to borrow your car again," Blackburn asked, "when could I?"

"For this long, you mean?"

"Yes sir."

The minister thought for a few moments.

"I suppose tomorrow," he said. "Though that might change."

Blackburn nodded.

"Do you want me to drive you up to the cottage?"

"No sir. There's light enough."

You got to be absolutely certain before doing anything else. That thought had troubled Blackburn more and more in the last hour. Maybe it was his injured head or his weariness, but once at the cottage, the clarity he'd had at the Clarkes' farm was seeping away. Blackburn looked down at the Hamptons' house. He thought not just of the lies but about Mr. Hampton poking the toe of his shoe to mark Naomi's grave site, Mrs. Hampton offering a five-dollar bill for digging the grave itself. In a rage, Blackburn went to the shed for a crowbar, tarp, and shovel.

The moon was out, its light silvering the stones and grass. Blackburn placed the vase and urn next to the lantern. *But nothing's decided yet,* Blackburn told himself. *You can shovel the dirt back in, say you're reseeding the plot.* Tired as he was, it felt good to hold the shovel, hurl gouts of dirt onto the tarp. This was something that didn't need thought, only doing. After each pitch, the shovel's blade caught moonlight, held its gleam before plunging back into the earth.

Blackburn's fury began to slow. He thought of what Mr. Clarke had said about choices. But even seven hours away from here, Blackburn knew he'd always live with the fear of being found out. Surely a time would come when Annie Mae would want to visit her father's grave. Could she be talked out of it, or at least convinced to make the pilgrimage

in secret? Blackburn stopped digging. He looked at the stones
that surrounded him. This also was a future. He thought of
what Wilkie had said about living with the dead too long.

Blackburn didn't stop again until it was time to enter the
grave. As he paused, the lack of food and sleep not so much
caught up to Blackburn as seized him, so much he wondered
if he'd have the strength to lift himself out once in. He could
get the ladder, but the effort to walk that far . . . Blackburn
looked around at the markers, the iron fence that contained
them, then down the hill toward the Hamptons' house.

He climbed in. The soil was more compressed now, the
added weight on the shovel blade noticeable. As he resumed,
Blackburn pondered what Naomi would want. But he knew
the answer to that. *Your Daughter,* she had written on the back
of the photograph. Yet what would be best for Annie Mae?
And who best to decide? He thought of how seldom Jacob
mentioned the child. Maybe the baby wasn't fully real to him.
How could it be when, unlike Blackburn, Jacob had never
held out a hand and felt its existence.

When his chin was even with the ground, Blackburn
paused. The casket was inches beneath him. Everything
seemed to be waiting, moon and stars, the encircling stones.
Blackburn pressed the blade tip in, struck wood. After scraping dirt off the coffin lid, Blackburn made room to set his feet.
He tossed the shovel onto the grass, reached for the lantern
and crowbar. He angled the crowbar under the lid's nearer
side. Wood creaked and the first nail gave. He pried free the
other nails, then those on the top and end board. *Naomi is
not in here. She is not,* Blackburn told himself. He placed the
lantern closer, turned the brass wheel. The flame expanded

inside the globed glass. "Forgive me if I'm wrong," he said aloud. Blackburn crouched, set the heel of his palm under the coffin lid, and pushed upward. The nails on the opposite side gave and the coffin yawned open.

Blackburn lifted the lantern. A wool blanket, something wrapped inside. He hesitated, then freed the blanket. Beneath, two burlap sacks leaked sawdust. After setting the lantern and crowbar on the grass, Blackburn gathered his strength and struggled out of the grave.

As he stood amid the silent stones, he did not think of the future but of the past: two boys clasping hands across a barbed-wire fence, an agreement sealed by blood. He snuffed the lantern, left the tools where they lay. A cardinal sang the world awake. First light sifted through the trees.

35

I T WAS DUSK WHEN BLACKBURN crossed the bridge. Mr. Clarke sat on the porch. He smiled and gave Blackburn a knowing nod before rising to open the door and tell Naomi she had a visitor. Holding Annie Mae in her right arm, Naomi came onto the porch, saw Blackburn, and hurried down the steps. She placed her free hand on his back, pressed the side of her face into his chest and kept it there. He felt Naomi's tears dampen his shirt, heard the child's breaths.

"I've been ever so worried," Naomi said, hugging him harder. "When I got to you, you were knocked out. I waited till you opened your eyes. I didn't want to leave, but I had to."

"I know."

"Lila said you'd tell the Hamptons and they'd come for Annie Mae. I didn't think it but I was still scared. I've missed you, Blackburn. I kept thinking you'd come, and now you have."

The baby began to fuss and Naomi stepped back, nudged the child higher on her shoulder.

"Ain't she an angel?"

"She is," Blackburn said.

"Got Jacob's hair color and nose," Naomi said, "but she has my eyes, don't you think?"

The child's eyes were indeed blue. Yet Naomi's eyes were different from the last time Blackburn had seen her. The same color but less sparkle, muted. After all she'd endured these last months, how could they not be.

Mr. Clarke stepped off the porch.

"I'm going to check on that calf before it's full dark," he said. "Why don't you all go in. You got a lot of catching up to do."

Blackburn followed Naomi inside. On the table, a lamp was already lit.

"Your daddy, he didn't tell you I come yesterday, did he?"

"Why, no, he didn't say nothing about that," Naomi answered, her smile lessening, but only for a moment. "But that don't matter. You're here now and we'll have us such a fine time catching up. You've got to stay for supper and the night. I'll not abide no for an answer."

"I need to tell you some things," Blackburn said. "Real important things."

"Is it about Annie Mae?" she asked, smile vanishing.

"It affects her. Something good but it ain't going to be easy to understand."

"You're scaring me, Blackburn."

"I ain't meaning to."

"Let me nurse Annie Mae and get her asleep," Naomi said after a few moments, and took the baby into the back room.

Blackburn listened to the night sounds. They seemed to settle deeper into a valley, hold longer than on the cemetery's ridgetop. He imagined the sounds—their aliveness—seeping into the soil, nurturing. In a few minutes, Mr. Clarke came up the steps. Soon after, the rocking chair began to creak. Blackburn looked out the window, saw only darkness. Naomi came back and sat down.

"Whatever you're needing me to know," Naomi said, "first tell me again it's something good."

"It is good, but getting to where you see it that way . . . Well, you got to hear me out to understand."

Blackburn began, but soon Naomi's face filled with anguish.

"I seen his grave and tombstone, I touched them. Why are you saying these things, Blackburn? Why?"

Outside on the porch, the chair stopped rocking, but the front door remained closed.

"Look at me," Blackburn told her, waiting until Naomi's eyes met his. "That day you put my hand where I could feel Annie Mae, I vow with this same hand," Blackburn said, holding it out, "that Jacob is alive. His parents lied, told Jacob you and the baby died. That grave you went to, they told him it was where you was buried. They told me and Dr. Egan the same."

He told her more. Gradually, doubt became belief.

"I got to be alone a few minutes," Naomi said.

She went into her and Annie Mae's room and closed the

door. A bucket scraping a dry well's bottom, that was what Blackburn felt like. Nothing left to offer up. He wanted to place his forearms on the table, close his eyes, and sleep more than three hours. He wanted stillness, calm, most of all inside his own heart.

When Naomi returned, she set a hand on the table's surface. Her fingertips brushed over the wood, as if gauging its smoothness.

"And Jacob didn't know what they done until just today?" Naomi asked when she looked up. "Not ever a hint nor suspecting."

"No."

"You're certain."

"I am," Blackburn answered. "He didn't believe me until I showed him what was in your coffin."

"I can't hold the all of it in my heart, Blackburn," Naomi said.

But Blackburn knew she was wrong, that the heart can hold so very much.

"I want to see him," Naomi said. "I'll just need a few minutes to pack and change Annie Mae's hippin. . . ."

"You got no need to do that."

Blackburn lifted the lantern off its nail. He took a match from the fireboard, lit the wick, and told Naomi to get Annie Mae. When Blackburn opened the front door, the rocking chair remained still. Blackburn held up the lantern and Naomi followed with Annie Mae in her arms. Once in the yard, Blackburn raised the lantern higher, swayed it side to side. Truck beams turned on in answer. They heard him coming, watched as Jacob splashed through the creek and into the yard. As Jacob and Naomi embraced, the child between them, Blackburn set the lantern at their feet and walked back onto the porch.

"I need to talk to you," Blackburn said.

"You ain't got a damn thing I want to hear," Mr. Clarke answered.

"I think you're wrong about that."

CODA

FOUR MONTHS LATER Blackburn sits on the cottage steps and gazes out at the cemetery's center. As the grass and trees darken, the two marble stones recede. A third grave plot is there, its ground twice dug, now twice filled. Blackburn's duties to the dead are done. The bus to Tennessee leaves early and he needs to finish packing, but he lingers. He looks down the hill. Where the Gulf sign had been, a yellow Shell emblem now hangs. In the front window, neon letters spell out *Hartley's Store*. The Hamptons' porch light is on. Jacob vowed never to set foot inside his parents' house again, so sent Blackburn to retrieve Naomi's letters from the bedroom drawer. All else abandoned. Blackburn suspects Mr. and Mrs. Hampton keep the bedroom as Jacob left it. Everything in its rightful place, as if even now expectant of return.

He wonders when he will see Jacob and Naomi again. Mr. Clarke had spoken some harsh words that evening Jacob appeared, as Lila had weeks later when Naomi announced they were moving to Louisiana for a fresh start. Nevertheless,

Mr. Clarke's love for Annie Mae eased tempers before Jacob and Naomi left. Unlike with the Hamptons, a breach that can be repaired.

Blackburn turns his thoughts to the future, the land he and Mr. Clarke will be clearing. It will be hard work—trees felled, stumps uprooted, rocks hauled away, but Blackburn has done such work before. It is, as Mr. Clarke said, in his blood. Blackburn imagines fields asleep beneath a veil of snow. Awaiting spring, awaiting him too, because he will be there, standing firm on broken ground to witness life rising into the light.

ACKNOWLEDGMENTS

Special thanks to Lee Boudreaux, Adam Eaglin, Beniamino Ambrosi. Elena Hershey, Cara Reilly, Kayla Steinorth, Melissa Yoon, Andrea Monagle. Kathy Brewer, Phil Moore, Brian Railsback, Tom Rash, Frédérique Spill, Randall Wilhelm, Ann, James, Caroline, Mackenzie, Joe, Collins.

RON RASH is the author of the 2009 PEN/Faulkner finalist and *New York Times* bestselling novel *Serena,* in addition to the critically acclaimed novels *The Risen, Above the Water-fall, The Cove, One Foot in Eden, Saints at the River,* and *The World Made Straight;* five collections of poems; and seven collections of stories, among them *Burning Bright,* which won the 2010 Frank O'Connor International Short Story Award, *Nothing Gold Can Stay,* a *New York Times* bestseller, and *Chemistry and Other Stories,* which was a finalist for the 2007 PEN/Faulkner Award. He is three times a recipient of the O. Henry Prize, and his books have been translated into seventeen languages. He teaches at Western Carolina University.